D0828695

"You may be deceived in me."

"With those eyes? I don't think so." Bruno brushed his thumb across the gentle swell of Louise's mouth. "Ninety-nine percent of the time I'm pathologically suspicious. The other one percent of the time, I'm totally trusting." He leaned back and considered her with amused, sexily narrowed eyes.

"But how do you *know* you can trust me?"

"I don't know," he said, shrugging. "I just do."

Louise bit her lip. If there was any real feeling growing between them, shouldn't she warn him? She stared mistily into his eyes. If she was to tell Bruno about the tape recorder, it must be now....

"What is it?" he asked. "There's suddenly a shadow in those eyes."

"Just a shadow, as you said." She smiled uncertainly.

Books by Madeleine Ker

HARLEQUIN PRESENTS

HARLEQUIN ROMANCE

These books may be available at your local bookseller.

Don't miss any of our special offers. Write to us at the following address for information on our newest releases.

Harlequin Reader Service
P.O. Box 52040, Phoenix, AZ   85072-2040
Canadian address: P.O. Box 2800, Postal Station A,
5170 Yonge St., Willowdale, Ont.   M2N 6J3

MADELEINE KER

---

fire of the gods

Harlequin Books

TORONTO • NEW YORK • LONDON
AMSTERDAM • PARIS • SYDNEY • HAMBURG
STOCKHOLM • ATHENS • TOKYO • MILAN

Harlequin Presents first edition June 1985
ISBN 0-373-10795-1

Original hardcover edition published in 1984
by Mills & Boon Limited

Copyright © 1984 by Madeleine Ker. All rights reserved.
Philippine copyright 1984. Australian copyright 1984.
Except for use in any review, the reproduction or utilization of
this work in whole or in part in any form by any electronic,
mechanical or other means, now known or hereafter invented,
including xerography, photocopying and recording, or in any
information storage or retrieval system, is forbidden without
the permission of the publisher, Harlequin Enterprises Limited,
225 Duncan Mill Road, Don Mills, Ontario, Canada M3B 3K9.

All the characters in this book have no existence outside the
imagination of the author and have no relation whatsoever to
anyone bearing the same name or names. They are not even
distantly inspired by any individual known or unknown to the
author, and all the incidents are pure invention.

The Harlequin trademarks, consisting of the words
HARLEQUIN PRESENTS and the portrayal of a Harlequin,
are trademarks of Harlequin Enterprises Limited and are
registered in the Canada Trade Marks Office; the portrayal
of a Harlequin is registered in the United States Patent
and Trademark Office.

Printed in U.S.A.

CHAPTER ONE

THE SICILIAN twilight was deeply, immensely peaceful.

Now that the sun had gone down, the fishermen's boats had been drawn up on to the shingles at Mazzaró, and of the crowds who had filled the baking beach by day, now only a few couples remained, enjoying the delicious hush, or gazing out to where the great white yacht rested calm and lovely on the burnished water, half a mile out to sea.

Its rigging had been pearled with fairy-lights, and the distant glitter made it alluring, like some magic thing about to set sail for an enchanted land.

'Besides,' Sophie Dubarry pointed out from her towel, 'you could treat it as part of your job. Take your cameras along to the party, and write an article about how the Beautiful People enjoy themselves.'

Louise, paddling in the blood-warm water, nestled into the shingle, enjoying the wet squeak of pebbles against her bikini-bottom, and surveyed her friend solemnly. The point of her chin was just above the water.

'You're way behind the times,' she reproved. 'Today's woman doesn't want to read about a bunch of decadent playboys. She wants her mind expanded. Facts, figures, interesting world events. Like the eruption of Europe's biggest active volcano.'

'Etna's not going to go up tonight,' Sophie said decisively. Pulling her curls away from her face, she turned to stare at the peak twenty miles away. Louise followed her gaze. So peaceful, that famous mountain, now etched against a violet sky. Only the red glow at the tip hinted at the titanic forces at work beneath the towering cone, still snow-clad despite midsummer. 'There haven't even been any tremors today.'

'If I miss the eruption, my editor will strangle me,' Louise protested. 'The first few minutes are crucial, Sophie—when the first big fireworks begin. After that the sky tends to get filled with ash and smoke up to seventy thousand feet high, and the light goes.' Two people walked past where Louise and Sophie had settled at the water's edge. Both were wearing publicity T-shirts. One read 'I LAVA VOLCANO', the other simply had a drawing of the famous cone, and the dates of the biggest recent eruptions. 'This is Europe's biggest free fireworks show,' Louise pointed out with a smile. 'When Mount Etna blows her top, she'll be on the front pages of the world's newspapers. If I miss out, *Women Today* will be left with egg all over its face—and I'll be out of a job.'

She had pulled her long, richly dark hair up into a chignon, out of the water's way, and now she rose from the waves like Aphrodite, and waded ashore, unfastening it as she went. Louise Jordan's elegant body was the essence of femininity—graceful, tanned golden by a week of Sicilian sun, and slender as a young gazelle. The handsome young men who'd been whistling at her tantalising figure ever since she'd arrived in Taormina last week would probably never realise that the green-eyed brunette with the velvety, kissable mouth was a talented photojournalist with growing experience in the field. Or that a hard-nosed editor in London regarded her as the most promising young photographer he'd ever employed.

The three cameras that were loaded and waiting in her straw bag weren't the usual tourist's equipment. Her assignment was to get the most dramatic possible photographs and story of the eruption that seismologists and vulcanologists agreed was now imminent. And *that*, despite the intoxicating lure of beach and nightlife, was what she was damn well going to do!

'Well,' Sophie Dubarry decided, "*I* want to go to the party.' Her own T-shirt, worn over faded jeans, read simply 'I LOVE A BIG BANG'. But then, in Louise's experience, neither French journalists in general nor her old friend Sophie Dubarry in particular were exactly renowned for their prudishness. 'For one thing,' Sophie went on dreamily, 'I'm dying to see what the yacht's like inside—they say it's a floating palace. And for another, Bruno Xavier happens to exert an uncanny spell over me.' She rolled brown eyes in a mock swoon. 'I might even become the first reporter in history to persuade him to grant an interview—and Bruno Xavier is a lot bigger news, in my book, than Etna erupting!'

Louise grinned at her friend's expression as she towelled herself dry. Her own black bikini was wickedly skimpy, and had been causing male blood-pressure in the vicinity to rise all day; but she was genuinely innocent about her beautiful and satiny body, and unselfconscious to an extent that sometimes raised Sophie's supposedly unshockable Gallic brows.

Anyway, Louise admitted freely that men had never interested her all that much—photography and journalism had been her first love since she was fourteen.

A sentiment which Sophie—who at twenty-three was a year older than her English colleague—did not share.

'You're not even tempted by the thought of meeting Bruno Xavier?' she queried in disbelief.

'Tempted, yes,' Louise admitted reluctantly. 'I must confess I'd like to go, if only to see how the other half live. But I'd never forgive myself if the volcano erupted while I was half a mile out to sea.' She pulled a towelling dress over her head, and shrugged it over her slim hips. 'Remember what happened at Mount St Helens? There were literally hundreds of photographers waiting for the eruption, day and night. And when the mountain eventually did go up, early one morning, no one was watching—except an amateur called Vern Hodgson, who scooped the most fabulous pictures ever.'

'Listen—Etna's always here. Bruno Xavier isn't! Besides,' Sophie protested, 'you'll have a magnificent view of Etna from the yacht,' She helped Louise gather up their things. 'That's apparently why he's moored the yacht there—to get a grandstand view of the eruption.'

'Exactly the sort of thing I don't like about the very rich,' Louise said disapprovingly. 'Treating an awesome natural phenomenon as an entertainment especially laid on for his benefit—the arrogance of it!'

'Isn't that what everyone else is doing?' Sophie asked practically, wincing as she brushed her tangled curls into some semblance of order.

'Some of us have to work for a living,' Louise retorted. She herself had just sent off the photographs and text of an article about the general excitement surrounding the predicted eruption. Since the first tremors and minor eruptions which had warned of the much bigger eruption to come, people had flocked from all over the world in the hopes of catching the fireworks—and despite the threat to their property from heavy ash fallout, the local villages were catering for this tourist bonanza with an atmosphere of exuberant holiday. Even the one or two places so close to Etna as to be threatened with extinction from the lava were excited and gay. And booming, not least with the presence of hundreds of international media people like herself, who would all be competing for the most spectacular pictures and words.

Still, she thought, looking wistfully at the glittering yacht off Mazzaró, she would love to go to the party. She'd never been aboard an ocean-going pleasure boat like *Merope*, and Sophie had been right—everyone who was anyone would be aboard tonight, enjoying Bruno Xavier's hospitality. David Lomax, through whom their invitation had come, swore that Xavier's hospitality was unrivalled—and as an ITV reporter for the past twenty years, he ought to know.

'Come on, Louise,' Sophie urged. 'We've only got an hour or so to get dressed. David's coming to pick us up at eight. Don't miss this party. You haven't even seen Bruno, have you?'

'I'm more interested in the yacht than in Bruno Xavier,' Louise said, still sounding disapproving. 'I don't like playboys.'

'He doesn't like journalists,' Sophie reminded her. 'Besides, Bruno isn't your average playboy. He's made every penny he's got, and he does actually work for a living, to use your somewhat censorious phrase!'

'I don't call barking down a telephone three times a day working for a living,' Louise rejoined. 'A man ought to work with his hands, even if it's only to push a pencil.' Her face was too lovely to hold a scowl for long, and her soft, wide mouth relented. 'But I agree that it does seem too good a chance to miss. But what if I lose out on Etna? The eruption will be even more spectacular at night.'

'Do what I said—take your cameras with you. Now, for the last time—will you come?'

'I may regret this,' Louise smiled. She slung the 35mm camera round her neck, and slotted the flashgun into its bracket. Always be prepared was the photographer's motto. '—but yes, I'm coming.'

'*Enfin,*' Sophie said happily. 'Shall we get the *autobus* back up to Taormina and get ready?'

Laughing, they made their way to the bus that would take them up the precipitously steep, winding road to the town.

The hotel that Percy Widows had booked Louise into had charmed her from the start, its peach-coloured walls and rococo furnishings suggesting a bygone age. Despite his grim exterior, her editor had an obvious soft spot for her, and had always made sure she got comfortable, if not luxurious, accommodation on overseas assignments. 'Learning your trade,' he had told her briefly, 'is best done in comfort.' Sophie, whose own Paris journal was rather more parsimonious, had been frankly envious—which didn't, of course, affect a friendship that went back to their schooldays. Sophie's English mother had decided that her daughter was to go to English schools, and she and Louise had been in the same class for three years.

Taormina had been the perfect choice of a base from which to monitor Etna. The beautiful town itself was set high up on the steep coastline, linked to the beach far below by a winding road full of hairpin bends, and lined with prickly pears, palms, and the burnt-orange roofs of villas. Etna was perfectly visible from almost anywhere, a symmetrical cone, always covered in cool snow—and was far enough away to be completely safe, something Louise had noted with relief.

Deciding on clothes for the party wasn't exactly a mind-bending problem. Louise had brought little but beachwear and light summer outfits, knowing what to expect of Sicily in July; she had a very feminine love of beautiful clothes and perfumes, though, and was regretting the infinitely more suitable dresses in her flat in London.

The dress she chose had been intended for casual evenings, but at a quick glance might just pass for something more elegant. The thin straps left her tanned shoulders bare, and the cool blue material set off her colouring well. In any case, she wasn't intending to make a grand appearance. Fitting in with the background was more what she had in mind, and maybe getting, as Sophie had recommended, a few pictures to mug up into a short article about Mediterranean high-life.

There was just time to wash and dry her hair. The heavy silken tresses were beginning to show golden hints from the sun already, but the effect wasn't displeasing. She studied herself without vanity in the mirror, thinking about the evening ahead. Bruno Xavier was a name she'd come across many times in her career, though she'd only seen him in photographs, and knew him only by reputation. And inexperienced a journalist as she was, Louise was fully conscious of the way reputations could lie. Rehearsing what little she knew about him, she realised that despite her vague disapproval earlier this evening, the only description she could come up with was a collection of strangely elusive clichés.

He had risen from childhood poverty, so the story ran, to become one of Europe's most successful businessmen by his early thirties. He had interests in steel, hotels, airlines, construction—many things that seemed to make him a lot of money. To judge by his photographs, he was darkly attractive. And obviously virile. Beneath the glamorous façade of yachts and expensive cars there remained enough of the ruthless poor-boy, the hard core of his motivation, to add spice to the image. The smouldering aggression that lay behind the urbane charm was famous, part of the legend. Newspaper editors, naturally, loved him. Even *Women Today* had run articles about him from time to time, emphasising the rags-to-riches story, which still exerted a powerful spell over readers' imaginations.

Louise pulled a face. That, too, might be just so much hype; rich men were able to manipulate the way other people thought about them. There was something in her that had always made her dislike the sound of Bruno Xavier. Perhaps she was just too cynical about legends and wilful playboys . . .

What else? she thought, brushing her hair. A generous man, known to like beautiful women. A man who played hard and worked hard. A man who could be dangerous. A fighter.

She squirted Opium at the hollow of her throat, and dabbed her pulses in the expensive sheen, revelling in the heady fragrance.

In the end, though, you were left with the clichés, because no one really knew what Bruno Xavier was like. The most persistent interviewers had bounced off that tough hide and dazzling smile. He simply didn't grant interviews. Ever. And their articles came down to the legends, for want of the truth. The legends and the beautiful women who surrounded him, the cars and yachts and the jewels and the private jets——

A different world altogether from her own peaceful

and orderly suburban upbringing.

She applied eyeshadow thoughtfully. The face that looked back at her from the mirror was honey-tanned, set in a frame of rich and darkly glossy chestnut hair. Green eyes, flecked with amber and emphasised by luxuriant eyelashes, a short, determined nose, a mouth made for smiling. That mouth was perhaps the most intriguing feature of her face; despite the kiss-inviting ripeness of her lips, there was an innocence about their slightly stubborn set that might have suggested to a sharply perceptive man—or an ordinarily perceptive woman—that very few men had kissed Louise Jordan with any real accomplishment. There was an un-awakened, vulnerable hint to her beauty, a naïvety which almost suggested that she didn't fully understand what it was that made the handsome young men on the beach whistle so persistently at her bikini-clad slenderness . . .

Completing her brief make-up with a fresh-looking red lipstick, she turned away to check her cameras for the evening ahead. She was going to take at least one telephoto lens just in case; carrying three cameras and assorted accessories around in an inelegantly large bag was an occupational drag she'd long since got used to.

She was just slipping sandals on to her bare feet, having decided that stockings probably weren't *de rigueur* in Sicily in the summer, even on Bruno Xavier's yacht, when the bedside phone rang to say that Sophie and David Lomax were waiting for her in their car outside.

With a smile of self-mockery, she discovered that her heart was beating a lot faster as she locked her door. Who knew what the night would bring? It was going to be interesting, anyway, to find out how Bruno Xavier lived, even if she wasn't going to get any further behind the urbane public image!

The moon had risen golden against a sky thick with stars by the time they were climbing from the motorboat on to the yacht's thronged stern. From shore, *Merope* had looked fairly big to Louise; once on board, it seemed huge. Both immaculate decks were thronged with people laughing, talking, and dancing. It was a bewilderingly glittering occasion; the sweet strains of the quartet in the stern were almost drowned out by the sound of merriment all around; feeling rather like Cinderella among all the minks and diamonds, Louise let David Lomax hijack drinks for her and Sophie from a passing steward, and gazed around with wide green eyes. The cameras in her bulky shoulder-bag were positively calling out to be used. The yacht was absolutely exquisite, all her brasswork gleaming and her woodwork spotless. Crushed between tuxedos and Paris gowns, she peeped through one of the windows into the huge stateroom.

'God,' David said in awe, 'will you take a look at that.'

The crowded room wasn't remotely nautical; the blazing chandelier was surely Clichy or Murano, and had probably come from the same *château* as the inlaid walnut panelling and the Louis XVI furniture. Only the great painting which dominated one wall, a dramatic storm at sea which might have been a Turner, suggested that this beautiful room had anything to do with shipboard life.

'I don't fancy my chances of getting that first-ever interview with Bruno Xavier in all this crowd,' Sophie smiled, taking in the sparkling throng with bright eyes.

With some inexplicable French insight, Louise noticed, she'd packed a very pretty silk dress, which was now showing her rather full figure off to perfection. She turned to David. 'Are they always like this?'

'Bruno's parties? Always.' Balding and dapper, David Lomax's pouchy-eyed face was vaguely familiar to millions through two decades of television reporting. Even his jaded susceptibilities, though, seemed a little stunned by the atmosphere of busy celebration on board this magnificent floating palace. 'But if you're thinking of trying to interview Bruno, young Sophie, make sure you have a life-jacket on. Because you'll definitely end up overboard! That's the Duchess of Amalfi,' he informed them in a lower voice, nodding at a group inside the stateroom. 'Half the aristocracy of Europe seems to be here tonight. I don't see our host, though . . .'

With a startling *whooosh*, a dozen rockets soared up into the night sky from the bridge, pouring gold sparks as they went. Her head thrown back to watch, Louise couldn't resist a smile of pure delight. At the dizzy height of their trajectory, the fireworks burst into scarlet and green and white blossoms of fire, expanding, then showering slowly downwards into the sea. An *'aaah'* of delight went up from the crowd as more rockets hissed their multicoloured way heavenwards. Louise looked at Sophie with dazzled eyes, and shook her head. 'I wouldn't have missed this for anything, Sophie! I'm glad you talked me into it.' She stared up at the flowers of light in the sky. 'Whatever else he may be, Signor Xavier certainly knows how to enjoy himself.'

Taking advantage of the distraction with a journalist's skill, David had fought his way to the buffet while the rockets went up, and now returned with plates heaped with caviare, olives, cold pheasant, and *paté de foie gras*.

'That's Bruno over there,' Sophie suddenly said in excitement, her mouth full. Louise gulped down caviare, and followed her friend's rapt gaze. A tall, dark haired man in a white dinner-jacket, his back to them, on the other side of the deck. A crowd of people had surrounded him, and the faces Louise could see were all laughing. Quickly, she pulled the Pentax out of her bag, and focused the 135mm lens on the group. It was a fascinating shot—the powerful man and his friends. That elegant white back, mysteriously turned away from the lens; the smiling faces, some amused, some worshipping, some with the glint of envy in their eyes——

She clicked the shutter, and focused again.

'Aren't you going to use flash?' David asked beside her.

'No.' Louise murmured against the camera. 'Too distracting in this situation.' She clicked again as another burst of laughter broke from the group. Bruno Xavier's hair, she noticed, was thick, a brazen invitation to female fingers. He turned slightly, showing her a glimpse of a bronzed profile, dark eyebrows, and a glint of white teeth. She clicked again, becoming fascinated by her quarry.

Then, with an abruptness that was like some sixth sense, he turned, and stared straight into Louise's lens. The shutter snapped out of pure reflex, and Louise's stomach suddenly somersaulted right over inside her, as though she'd stepped on to a high-voltage cable. She wasn't so much conscious of the rest of his face—it was those eyes that reached out to her, a physical shock to her emotions that almost jolted a gasp from her constricted throat. *Compelling*, she thought humbly. *My God, he could make anyone do anything for him . . .*

Then the contact was broken as he turned away, leaving her with the hint of an ironic gleam. She lowered the camera dazedly, realising that she'd just missed the portrait-shot of a lifetime. In that blazing second, Bruno Xavier's soul had reached out of his dark eyes—what colour were they? She didn't even remember—and had communicated something of the man's inner dynamism, his sheer male vitality. And she'd missed the shot.

Somehow, it didn't seem to matter. She blinked at Sophie Dubarry, who was shaking her arm.

'Louise? What the hell is wrong with you?'

'Nothing,' Louise said slowly.

'Why didn't you take another shot while he was looking our way?' she demanded.

'The——' She cleared her throat, looking at the camera in her hands. 'The shutter jammed,' she lied. But he hadn't just been looking their way. He had been looking at *her*, right into her soul, for all she knew, reading every secret there . . .

'*Mon Dieu*,' Sophie crooned, 'isn't he handsome? Now do you see what I mean?'

'I didn't notice his looks,' Louise replied, which was the literal truth, despite Sophie's wide-eyed disbelief. She turned to David. 'What colour are his eyes, do you know?'

'The girl's gone mad,' Sophie groaned.

'They're grey,' David said, watching Louise thoughtfully. 'A deep blue-grey. Didn't you notice?'

Louise shook her head, automatically winding on the next shot. All she remembered were those dark pupils, and the shock of the man's soul that had reached out to her for a second—powerful, ironic, mature. So sure of his own strength.

That contact had shaken her more than she could ever have expected possible. Sophie, still mooning over Bruno's indifferent back, didn't notice; but David Lomax's worldly-wise eyes showed concern.

'Have some more champagne, Lou. You look as though you've seen a ghost.'

'He's got the most riveting eyes I've ever seen,' Louise said quietly, accepting the tulip glass. She was beginning to feel that Sophie had been right—maybe there was an excellent photographic essay in the making here—not about the party, but about the host.

'Sure,' David said. 'Somehow one expects top people to be ordinary—millionaires and politicians and actors. They're not, of course; they're unique, which is why they make it to the top.' There was another burst of laughter from the group across the deck, and then the tall man disengaged himself gracefully, and made his way towards the prow, where another group eagerly welcomed him.

'The perfect host,' Sophie sighed. He hadn't looked their way again, to Louise's mingled relief and disappointment. She'd almost expected him to come over to them—but as her reactions cooled, her inbuilt scepticism reasserted itself slightly. Maybe she'd been over-impressed by that chance meeting of eyes? The 135mm lens, with its tendency to glamourise images, had probably given her a false impression. And the man probably hadn't noticed her at all.

'Anyway,' David smiled, 'let's circulate. I'll try and introduce you two to some interesting people.'

Joining in the amused chatter of the group David

introduced them to, she couldn't help remembering her delight when Percy Widows had thrown the Etna assignment her way. It hadn't just been that the thought of witnessing an eruption had been exciting; she'd also anticipated that a couple of weeks in Sicily were going to be something like an unexpected holiday. There was even an element of mystery, as no one could possibly predict when exactly the volcano was going to erupt. It might even take weeks.

But this trip had been full of unexpected bonanzas. The island, for one thing, had been more exquisitely beautiful than she'd dreamed, a romantic setting *par excellence*. Meeting Sophie, one of her oldest friends, had been another. And now this glamorous yacht-party!

Inevitably, the talk centred around two topics—Etna and Bruno Xavier.

'He was going to take the yacht on a cruise,' a bright young woman, who claimed some slight acquaintance with Xavier, told them eagerly, 'but now he's going to wait here and see Etna go up. Isn't it a *fabulous* idea?' She turned to Louise. 'You ought to know,' she said, 'reporters know everything! When's the mountain going to erupt?'

'I'm afraid I can't tell you,' Louise smiled. The tip of Etna was a tiny red spark in the distant night, and she stared at it thoughtfully. 'Nobody can. The scientists are doing their best to work out ways of predicting the exact moment, but they haven't got there yet.'

'It's all very exciting,' someone else put in. All these earthquakes and rumblings underground. Did you feel the one last week?'

'Frightening,' David Lomax agreed. 'All those rumblings and tremors mean that molten rock is slowly forcing its way up the throat of the volcano. There's a gigantic ocean of lava about a mile beneath the earth's crust, and every now and then it forces its way up the funnel. No one really knows why. When the pressure gets too great, the plug of solidified lava and ash from the last eruption will blow out.'

'And then,' Sophie finished with bright eyes, 'the fun will start.'

'If you want to call it fun,' David said with a wry smile. 'To me it's like the end of the world—a bit too Biblical to take lightly!'

'I agree,' Louise said. She shook her long, glossy hair back, her expression rapt. 'It's so incredibly primitive, isn't it? So awesome. Like a link with the Earth's ancient past. Etna's been spouting fire since prehistoric times—for millions of years, maybe. It scares me to think of all that molten lava deep underground, thrusting its way out. Just think how far down the funnel must go . . .'

'Still,' one of the men put in practically, 'Etna may be spectacular, but it's not all that dangerous. For one thing it erupts fairly regularly, so you don't get really fearsome pressures building up. For another thing, the magma is relatively fluid, so it doesn't block up the vent—which is what happened at Mount St Helens, in the U.S.A.'

'By God, that was a bang,' David nodded. 'As big as a nuclear explosion. Bigger than Pompeii.' As if to underline the conversation, another sheaf of rockets blazed their way into the sky, and exploded into colour high above.

'Bruno really knows how to throw a party,' someone laughed. Louise reached into her bag, and checked the Pentax.

'I'm going to wander around,' she told Sophie, 'and take some pictures. Percy might just be able to use them.'

'Sure,' Sophie nodded, the sparkle of the fireworks reflected in her brown eyes. Louise melted away, and walked alongside the rail, where the Mediterranean lapped quietly in the darkness. The sea air was pleasant on her silky arms and shoulders. A photographer's life, she reflected ironically, was one long gamble; when not actually on assignment, she seemed to spend most of her time taking pictures of anything and everything that happened, on the off-chance that Percy Widows might be interested.

The party was in full swing now, and she fitted the wide-angle lens on to take in the whole scene. Pure glamour, she smiled to herself, clicking and winding on. There must be more pearls and diamonds on this one yacht tonight than in the whole of Sicily! There was no sign of Xavier. No doubt he'd be in the stateroom, applying his formidable charm to whichever of those exquisite women he'd chosen to be his partner. *After* the party. The two decks were vivid with colour and light. If only she could get far enough away to take in the entire party ... She glanced upwards. The bridge was dark and deserted above, and there was a brass companion leading up. A tasseled silk rope had been strung across the landing, obviously intended to warn partygoers off. She looked around. No one was on hand to see or stop her, so she slung the Pentax round her neck, ducked under the rope, and climbed swiftly upwards.

The bridge was dark, the banks of dials and instruments gleaming softly. It was good to be out of the crush, too. She leaned over the rail, and focused downwards. Perfect. The lens was wide enough to take in the whole foredeck, right up to the flags that fluttered in the prow. The string of lights on the rigging above completed an exciting, sophisticated image. She took the shot, wound on, and snapped again. Good. With the automatic deftness of a professional, she slipped the wide-angle off the camera, and replaced it with the 200mm lens, which would be long enough to capture individual faces among the crowd.

It was a pity she couldn't use her flash-gun; but the distraction would irritate people, at least make them self-conscious. Still, the soft glow of the moon and the fairy lights was bewitching in its own way . . .

'Silken ropes, I see, are not enough.' The deep, velvety voice made her spin round with a gasp, her green eyes wide. She might have dropped the precious camera had it not been looped around her neck. Her heartbeat fluttered wildly. She hadn't even seen Bruno Xavier, lazily reclining in the captain's chair, his white jacket a pale blur in the darkness of the bridge. 'Still, I'm glad to see my party hasn't actually bored you,' he went on. The deep voice carried a trace of accent, a feral growl beneath the purr. 'At first I thought *ennui* must have driven you up here. But your interest reassures me.'

'I—I just came up here to take some photographs,' she stammered, her skin beginning to flush duskily. 'I didn't mean to intrude.'

'Of course you meant to intrude,' he contradicted calmly. 'Why lack the courage of your convictions?' He rose with a panther's grace, and stepped out of the shadows. 'Besides, it remains to be seen whether your intrusion is desirable or not. You're the woman who was photographing me earlier,' he decided, dark eyes studying her lazily. 'One of the two journalists who came with David Lomax. Not the Frenchwoman. So—Miss Jordan, I presume?'

Being able to recall trivial details like stranger's names was a trick many successful men had. It was impressive, nonetheless. 'Yes,' Louise said quietly, feeling her pulses settling slowly towards normality again, 'I'm Louise Jordan.' He was even taller than she'd realised, a big, powerful man whose beautifully cut clothes couldn't disguise the naked power that must lie beneath the fine cotton and raw silk. The fist which rested on one hip was veined and muscular, as though it hadn't been retired from brawling and battering all that long. The darkly virile face was familiar, yes—but the photographs had never captured the life of the man, the passion that smoked in the sea-grey eyes, the authority in that chiselled mouth, the aggressive mastery that burned in every expression, every movement. Facing him so close, she was almost physically aware, with that same initial shock, of the self-assurance in Bruno Xavier, the calm, ironic maturity that set him apart from every other man she'd ever known.

'In which case,' he said in that husky, velvety voice, 'may I welcome you aboard my yacht, Louise Jordan.' Rather dazedly, she surrendered her hand to him, blinking at the touch of his lips against her smooth skin. Coming to, she snatched her fingers away with a haste that was almost rude.

'Thank you, Signor Xavier. And now, if you'll accept my apologies, I'll rejoin my friends——'

'Not so fast.' The smile was little more than an enigmatic quirk of bronzed lips, but the long fingers which closed around her cool arm were a lot more definite. She gazed helplessly up into those smoky eyes, as coolly unexpected against the bronzed face as dawn at sea. 'You've trespassed against *Merope*'s law, Louise Jordan. I still have to determine a fit punishment for your disobedience.' The accent was intriguing, half-French, half-Italian, but Louise felt naïvely unsure how serious the banter was.

'Punishment?' she repeated, her mouth uncertain.

'Indeed.' His eyes searched the honeyed skin of her face, probing the rock-pool depths of her eyes, lingering on the crushed rose-petal satin of her lips. 'You're a ward of court, I'm afraid, until I reach my decision.'

Dismay made Louise succumb to the arrogance without a retaliatory shot. The hard fingers slid possessively round her elbow as he turned her round to look down at the crowded deck beneath them. Was it the man's aura that had turned her nervous system into an electrified circuit? Or was she simply responding to the mythology that surrounded Bruno Xavier? Hard to tell, she admitted, feeling the mahogany deck like quicksand beneath her feet. This delicious rollercoaster terror had imprisoned her tongue, and the warm, expensive smell of him touched her in some directly primitive way.

'Now tell me,' he said softly, his eyes intent on the oblivious partygoers below, 'what makes this scene so photographically interesting to a young reporter?'

She mustered her senses with a deep breath. 'Glamour,' she said, glancing at the hawk-fierce profile beside her. Her fluttering heartbeat made her own voice sound uneven, and she cursed her own weakness, and searched for poise. 'Not everyone lives like this, Signor Xavier,' she said, aiming gentle malice at the almost melancholy irony she could somehow sense in him. 'To most people, this is all just a dream.' She waved slim fingers at the throng below. 'All I do is parcel it up in a handful of glossy prints, and my editor sells it to them.'

'So. You are a seller of dreams.' The dark brows dipped infinitesimably, changing the whole mood of his face in some strange way. 'Which magazine do you work for?'

'*Women Today*.'

'You will forgive me,' he purred, turning to look into her eyes again, 'if I confess that I've never heard of it.' The shock of his stare rendered her suddenly dry-mouthed and giddy.

'It—it's quite a respected magazine,' she offered. Damn him! Was he able to turn the voltage on and off, like some kind of machine? Dear God, women must look like X-ray plates to him, all ribs and thudding hearts and unhideable excitement.

'It would be,' he drawled. 'I trust that your respected editor hasn't sent you all the way to Sicily in pursuit of me?'

'Not quite,' she replied hastily, unsettled by the hint of aggression in him. 'I've come to photograph the eruption.'

'Ah. Forgive my vanity.' Again, she caught that strange hint of self-mockery in the man, the sense of disillusionment and sardonic humour. He'd probably grown too jaded with wealth and power, she thought primly. 'Our own little gateway to Hell,' he said softly, glancing at the red worm in the distance that was Etna. The band at that moment struck up a lively waltz, and excited laughter rose up from the crowd as people spun in impromptu dance. 'There's something about an imminent volcanic eruption that seems to cheer people up,' he observed with barbed amusement in that velvety voice. 'As though they were dancing on the edge of the world. It's a kind of *Götterdämmerung*, a twilight of the gods.' His fingers caressed her arm absently, savouring the silken skin. Wishing that he'd stop, and let her pulse-rate settle back to normal, Louise shook her head decisively.

'Not at all. It's just a big fireworks display. And the effect of vintage Bollinger,' she added. The sensual touch had unleashed butterflies in her stomach, their gauzy wings finding nerves she never even knew she had. 'If you'll forgive me, signor,' she ventured, 'you sound rather disillusioned with your own party.'

'Why do you say that?'

'Well,' she countered, 'why are you brooding alone up here, like—like Satan on the parapets of Notre Dame?'

His laugh was a brief rumble, to Louise uneasily reminiscent of Etna. 'You find me Satanic, Louise Jordan?'

'Not exactly,' she replied. There was fascination, bewitching passion, in the curve of his lips, and she tore her green eyes away with difficulty. 'I just wonder what makes a very rich, very successful man retreat in the middle of his own party and sit alone in the dark.'

'A pool of peace in a desert thronged with people,' he suggested obliquely. He met her wide-eyed gaze, his dark lashes veiling a slow smile. 'Why do you look at me like that? Are you going to turn this encounter into an article?'

'Oh no,' she said quickly. 'But,' she went on, 'I'd be very grateful if——'

'If?'

'If you'd let me take a portrait shot of you.'

'Right now? My dear Miss Jordan,' he said, pronouncing her name in the French way, 'a million portraits have been taken of Bruno Xavier. What makes you think yours will be any different?'

'Because now,' she said impulsively, deciding on utter frankness, 'your famous defences are temporarily down, signore. Maybe if I take you now, something of the real Bruno Xavier will show up in the picture.'

'The real Bruno Xavier,' he repeated in amusement. His gaze took in the wild-honey tan of her arms and slim throat, the eagerness of eyes as clear as cabochons, her lips parted in expectation. *'Allora,'* he shrugged. 'Do your worst.'

'Thank you,' she said in heartfelt delight, and dug into her bag for the Hasselblad. The big camera was much more bulky and inconvenient than the Pentax, but its unmatchable lens and large-size negatives were superb for portrait work. 'Just stay there,' she begged.

'There's nowhere to escape to,' he pointed out with a touch of acrid humour. If she could only capture that self-mocking, world-weariness . . .

She focused with pounding heart, determined not to miss a great photograph for the second time that night. How powerful his neck was, how classically beautiful the set of his head on broad shoulders. He was leaning against the rail on one arm, long fingers laced over his flat midriff. The soft light caressed the skin of his face, picking up the wine-red rose in one lapel——

'Satisfied?' he asked. One eyebrow curved sardonically as he spoke. Without thinking, Louise released the shutter.

'There,' she whispered. Only development would tell, but she was certain in her veins that the picture would be at least intriguing, possibly unique!

'And now,' he said, straightening, 'it's time I rejoined my guests.' Disappointment stabbed unexpectedly through her as the intimate, faintly melancholy mood evaporated. He adjusted the rose in his lapel, and this time his eyes were warm, smiling down at her with a mature sexiness that was like cognac in her veins. This man, her mind told her sharply, has stepped right out of a time when men were men and women just didn't matter a damn! He probably hadn't even heard that women had the vote . . .

'I hope you manage to sell your dream,' he said. 'In the meantime, the court has reached its decision regarding your crime.' Beautiful teeth glinted in a quick smile. 'Before I execute sentence, Miss Jordan, I feel I should read you a little sermon: don't wander past barriers. Not even silken ropes. Sometimes they aren't there just to keep people out—but to keep something else *in*. Understood?' She nodded mutely, and he stepped forward. 'And this is your penalty.'

She was so astounded at the firm contact of his lips that she simply stood rigid, clutching her ungainly bag. It was a warm, amused kiss, that lasted just a second longer than was necessary to melt every bone in her body. Man kisses woman, she thought insanely. As simple and as cosmic as that.

She stared up into his face with misty green eyes, as though she'd glimpsed some remote, hitherto unsuspected continent in the dawn. Grey eyes glinted back at her. 'Case dismissed,' he smiled. And as though he was completely unaware of the havoc he'd just unleashed in Louise Jordan's heart, he turned to walk down the companionway to the bright crowds below.

He didn't turn to look back.

Slowly, she replaced the Hasselblad in its case, dazed excitement was still flickering along her arteries. Only that little square of celluloid in the Hasselblad carried any record of this strange meeting.

No—there was something more. His kiss was still warm on her lips, like sunlight on a rose. If there were only some way of reproducing *that* image, she thought with a smile, Louise Jordan would be a rich woman. Except that she'd never sell his kiss, not for a million. It had been too sweet, too heart-stoppingly real.

Down below, the white-jacketed figure was again the centre of an eager crowd. She caught the rumble of his laugh above the music and chatter, and knew that she'd been utterly forgotten. She drew a long, shaky breath, and started climbing down. Would Sophie ever believe what had happened? When she saw that picture, she'd be consumed with professional and feminine jealousy! Suddenly swept up in the magic of the evening, Louise went to find her friend.

CHAPTER TWO

RICCARDO CERVELLO, Indian-dark, and heavily be-
spectacled from twenty years of poring over photographic prints in artificial light, straightened up. 'It's a
remarkable picture,' he said, shaking his grizzled head.
'That expression—quite haunting.'

Louise, excited to the point of having dusky roses in her
cheeks, had to agree. 'It's come out well,' she said
modestly. The ten by twelve colour print was still damp
from the fixer, but it was outstandingly good. The irony in
that magnificently handsome face flavoured the whole
photograph with a pungent, smoky melancholy. The light
had been perfect, emphasising the virile classicality of
Bruno Xavier's features, softly hinting at the luxury of the
background. Yet for all the glamour inherent in the
photograph, it had somehow captured the sensitive
interior of the man in a way no other picture she'd seen
had ever managed. When you studied those eyes, you saw
a complex, powerful man. Not just a face. They were both
sad and harsh, laughing and grim, incontrovertibly *alive*.
A shiver of gooseflesh crossed her brown arms.

'The 35mm prints are equally good,' Riccardo said,
picking them up delicately. His Catánia laboratory had
long handled all the rush jobs that the international
news community needed doing, and it was a bare two
days since the night of the party. The prints *were* good,
though nothing like as piercingly real as the single
portrait of Xavier. Rich people dancing, laughing, being
beautiful. Good, but not unique.

'Riccardo,' she said quickly, 'could you print another two of the Xavier portrait?'

'Sure,' he nodded. 'Everything's set up—I'll do them now. Can you wait half an hour?'

'I'll be back,' she promised, scooping up the pictures he'd already printed. 'There's just time to get these to the courier on this afternoon's London flight. If I can persuade some taxi-driver to break the law.' Leaving the darkroom wizard to get back to his chemicals, Louise ran down the stairs, sliding the prints into a manila envelope. Percy would have these by tonight; with luck, they could be in the next *Women Today*, due out at the weekend.

In the taxi to the airport, she flipped out the Xavier portrait, and studied it again. She couldn't stop the squirm of excited delight in her stomach. Superb! One of the best, most moving portraits she'd ever taken. The enigmatic smile on that sensuous mouth reminded her sharply of the kiss he'd left her with, and the excitement inside her took on a distinctly warmer glow.

For a woman who'd been keeping men at a cool, amused distance for the past five years, she was succumbing to this masculine magic with undignified ease! Why worry? she shrugged, and smiled blissfully out at the Sicilian sunlight. She wasn't likely to see Bruno Xavier ever again, and it was nice to have a romantic dream or two around the place. For a change. She'd always been vaguely uncertain about her own sensuality, a kind of intimate shyness which she needed to disguise under cool professionalism.

Not that men hadn't been tempted to melt that glacial exterior; ice-green eyes and plum-ripe lips had caused more than one colleague to ask her out, and subsequently lose his dignity, if not his heart. She'd looked on, her essential shyness undissolved, and had explained it all to herself by deciding that some people needed a lot of it, and some didn't. She had to be one of those who didn't. *It*. Shuddering ecstasy, heavy breathing, all the things she read about or saw on screens. A strange pleasure that some women seemed to take in having their breasts mauled, or their lips crushed.

Who needs *that*? she wondered, scrambling out of the taxi, and making for the courier's office in the echoing airport building. When Mother Nature had devised the processes of reproduction and physical love, she had surely been in a very silly mood. Now, if men all kissed the way Bruno had done, firm, warm, velvety, commanding—there might be some profit in it . . .

She was just in time to catch the courier. Slightly breathless, she licked the flap, sealed the envelope, and scribbled Percy Widows' name on it.

The courier, a dignified young man who cultivated a responsible expression, found his thoughts wandering alarmingly at the sight of Louise's pink tongue and panting breasts. Sicily, he told himself bitterly, was enough to wreak mischief on the self-control of a saint. He accepted the envelope, and added it to his collection of deliveries.

'Will you manage to get it to *Women Today* by tonight?' she pleaded. 'It's very important.'

'I'll do my best.' He responded glumly to Louise Jordan's wave, and studiously averted his gaze from her trim brown calves as she walked out of his office. Lady journalists. He was looking forward to the gloom of Heathrow, and the respectable, middle-class seclusion of Ponder's End.

Acting on impulse, Louise put another of the portrait prints into an envelope, and sent it, with no message, to Bruno Xavier, on *Merope*.

Over lunch she showed the other to Sophie Dubarry with a mischievous grin.

'Like my latest pin-up?'

Sophie's shriek caused the entire restaurant to stare their way. Oblivious, she gaped with stunned brown eyes at the glossy photograph.

'*Mais, c'est incroyable!* Where the *hell* did you take this picture, you green-eyed vixen?' She stared closer. 'That's the yacht!' She looked up at Louise's face. 'It was true! All that yarn about meeting Bruno on the bridge—you really did do it!'

'Why should I deceive you?' Louise asked virtuously. Sophie shook her curly head, and held the picture up reverently.

'This is just magnificent, Lou. I've never seen such a——' She hesitated. 'Such an *intimate* portrait. You've really got under his skin. Look at the tiredness in that smile, the cynicism. Who'd have thought he really felt like that,' she marvelled.

'I'm glad you like it,' Louise said, pushing her plate away.

'Like it?' Sophie echoed, at last looking up. 'I love it. It's beautiful.' She tapped her midriff. 'It hits me right there, Lou. So much feeling, so much mood . . .' With a wry smile, she aimed an imaginary gun at Louise. 'Own up—how on earth did you get him to pose like that?'

'I just asked,' Louise said. 'He was in a strange mood—as though he'd needed to escape from the party and just rest for a while.' She shrugged. 'I guess I was lucky enough to be in the right place at the right moment. That's how some of the best pictures get taken.'

Sophie rested her pointed chin on clasped hands, and studied the picture intently. 'You're becoming an artist, Lou. No, don't be silly,' she said, interrupting Louise's protest. 'You really are. Over the past two years you've picked up so much skill, it's unbelievable. Percy's lucky to have you, you know. With stuff like this,' she tapped the print, 'you could be syndicating your work world-wide. As it is, Percy will probably be able to sell this to every magazine in Europe and America.'

'Which would be a nice bonanza for me,' Louise smiled, watching the highlights glint on Sophie's curls, and remembering her friend at sixteen, tempestuous mixture of tomboy and shameless flirt, with the same untidy curls dancing in the same captivating way.

'Weren't you even nervous when you took this shot?' Sophie queried.

'Only a little,' she confessed. 'Why should I be nervous?'

'If it had been me, I'd have been shaking in my shoes! I mean—*Bruno Xavier* . . .'

'He's just a rich man,' Louise protested. 'Not some kind of god.'

'Still that English *sang-froid*,' Sophie sighed. 'It's very hard to believe that you didn't have some kind of special *rapport* with the man when you took this shot.'

'Well, I didn't!'

'And very difficult to escape the conclusion that you're taking this whole episode in a very happy-go-lucky way. Contrary to your protestations, Bruno is *not*

your Mr Average.' She shook a finger under her
friend's nose. 'You just be careful, Miss Jordan. One
day your nonchalance will land you in hot water.'
Reluctantly, she surrendered the print, her eyes
following it wistfully as Louise slipped it back into the
envelope.

'Or hot lava, maybe.' Louise swivelled in her chair,
and glanced at the calm white cone of Etna in the
distance. Only a smudge of grey smoke against the
cobalt sky suggested the trapped hellfire beneath.
'Which brings us back to a rather more reluctant
photographic subject. When *is* this mountain going to
perform?'

'I phoned the monitoring station on Etna just before
lunch,' Sophie said. 'I think they're getting a bit sick of
people wanting to know when Etna's going to perform.
Anyway, according to Curi it could be tonight, next
week, or next month.'

'Helpful.'

'He did point out something else,' Sophie added,
looking thoughtful. 'The longer the eruption takes to
begin, the more violent it's likely to be. The fact that it's
taking so long probably means that huge pressures are
building up.'

'That did occur to me,' Louise sighed. The cool white
peak teased her, as unapproachable as Fate. 'The sort
of eruption everyone wants is the usual thing—
spectacular fireworks, streams of lava, an impressive
cloud. But I'm not sure I want to be around if there's
going to be a Krakatoa-type bang!'

'Anything,' Sophie shrugged, 'so long as I can get
some kind of a story back to Paris. My editor's
beginning to make snide remarks about keeping
expensive journalists on paid holiday in the sun.'

'That's probably just what Percy's thinking,' Louise agreed with a smile. 'So—where are we going to wait for Etna today? The beach?'

'The beach,' Sophie grinned, stooping to tug a sandal-strap straight. Abruptly, she was sitting on the floor, her mouth opening in a surprised laugh.

Their table, absurdly, slid across the stone floor. There was a shattering of glass, and Louise's mind tilted as she found herself staggering backwards helplessly, wondering insanely how much wine she'd drunk.

The vibration began deep underground, a shudder that seemed to shake the very core of the earth. Screams and smashing crockery were drowned out as the shudder became a steady, brain-shaking roar. In terror, Louise grabbed Sophie's shoulders, trying to shelter her friend's head from the rain of plaster and masonry that filled the air. *This can't be happening*, she told herself in disbelief, clinging to Sophie. Her very teeth were rattling in her head, and someone was trying to tear the framework of the room apart. It was as though an unimaginably vast fist were shaking the building like a child's toy. She knew they should run out of the building in case the quake collapsed it like a house of cards, but she couldn't leave Sophie.

Then, slowly, the tremors receded. There was a moment of hush, another dying shudder, and then peace. Screams and nervous laughter accompanied a general clatter of people shaking crockery out of their laps and emerging from under tables.

'*Un terremòto,*' one of the waiters said with a slightly shaky laugh, picking plaster out of his hair.

'An earthquake,' Sophie echoed, her own face dusty. Louise grabbed her precious bag, and ran to the balcony. The calm white cone in the distance was unmoved. In the street below, people were laughing and joking in a mixture of excitement and relief. Nothing seemed to have fallen down, though the mediaeval Taormina streets were littered with roof-tiles.

'No eruption,' she said, turning back to Sophie.

'Don't sound so disappointed,' Sophie reproved, her face showing obvious relief. She swatted dust off her clothes, an occupation that the rest of the restaurant was now engaged with, sharing the gay *bonhomie* that follows a not-too-serious moment of terror. 'That was the biggest yet!'

'I thought it was the wine,' Louise confessed. They both giggled with a touch of hysteria. The restaurant was unharmed, though most of the ceiling plaster had ended up in the patron's dinners, and a lot of the crockery was now on the floor. No one seemed unduly affected, and the manager, apparently used to taking such things in his stride, was proclaiming free wine all round.

She checked her cameras, found all well, and slotted the wide-angle lens on to the Pentax. The restaurant made an interesting and amusing picture, and she took half a dozen frames. With characteristic Sicilian *bravura*, everyone was making the most of the manager's offer, apparently oblivious to the fact that the red wine among the piles of plaster on the tables could just as easily have been blood.

'Well,' Sophie observed as they picked their way to the exit, 'things are hotting up at last. I wonder if a largish earthquake merits a paragraph or two?'

'Maybe we'd better do some real work this afternoon,' Louise nodded. 'But let's have a quick swim first—okay?' Grit and dust had found its way under her clothes, and she was itching for the sea. Not just to get the plaster off—but for spiritual reasons as well. That had been a close shave, and her imagination was too vivid to let her simply laugh it away. She wanted to wash the hint of death off her body.

They were slightly subdued on the bus down to the beach, but the swim was deliciously reviving. Waving goodbye to Sophie an hour later, Louise walked up the street to her hotel. They'd both decided that the experience might merit a short filler article. She rehearsed the events in her mind, moving backwards through the terror to the ludicrous detail of Sophie sitting on the floor with a laugh. Odd, that muzziness in her head just before the quake. Had it been a kind of premonition? She dismissed the thought, and went to find out whether the peach-coloured plaster in her room was still intact.

She had been awake for a few minutes the next morning, and was revelling in the cool air from her opened shutters, when the maid tapped at her door with a cup of coffee and her mail—a single telegram from London, which she knew would be from Percy Widows.

She turned the taps on for a bath, and climbed back into bed with her coffee-cup and the telegram and tore the envelope open.

Your Xavier portrait magnificent, it read. *Am holding publication pending intimate full-length article and photographic essay on Bruno Xavier. Text about 5,000 words. As soon as possible please. Absolutely unique opportunity here for your career. Xavier is excellent copy.*

Emphasise human element of subject, romantic interests, emotional involvements, etc. Try and get details of Laura Ackermann affair, business and personal plans for future.

This ought to keep you out of mischief till Etna erupts, though judging by portrait you've been in mischief already?

Please cable if you need funds etc. Were you hurt in earthquake? Repeat Xavier photo excellent. Well done, best wishes, Percy.

Louise let her breath out with an explosive sigh. An intimate article on Bruno Xavier? And how did Percy imagine she was going to get *that*? Only through an interview—and it was well-known throughout the publishing industry that Bruno Xavier actively hated giving interviews! He hadn't given one in ten years, and there had been at least one violent clash with a too pressing reporter, who'd wound up with a black eye and a squashed microphone.

Didn't Percy realise she'd already achieved the impossible in getting that shot?

But Percy had obviously got the impression from the pictures that she and Bruno were in some way friendly. *Intimate.* She shook her head rather ruefully at the telegram. The Widows mind was obviously imagining all kinds of goings-on under the volcano. Still, this was serious. A command from Percy Widows was not to be lightly ignored. She couldn't simply row out to the yacht, though, and demand to be made privy to all of Bruno Xavier's secrets!

Such as Laura Ackermann, whoever she was. A fiancée? Lover? Business partner?

She drank her coffee thoughtfully. Percy's excitement

was understandable. That portrait suggested some kind of insight, some special relationship. The journalist who could truly draw Bruno out of his shell and offer even a glimpse of the real man behind the image would have an instant success on his hands. In-depth interviews were the most difficult kind of journalistic art, and really good ones with very private people like Bruno were worth their weight in diamonds.

But how on earth was she going to get so close to Bruno again? That moment on the yacht had been unique, a once-in-a-lifetime coincidence.

She picked up her hairbrush, and started brushing her hair peacefully, waiting for the bath-tub to fill. She'd simply have to tell Percy that there wasn't a chance ... The bedside telephone rang, and she picked it up.

Her mood of tranquil relaxation exploded in a second as a familiar, husky voice purred into her ear.

'Good morning, Miss Jordan.'

'Signore Xavier?' The coincidence was startling, to say the least! Breathless all of a sudden, she dropped her brush and held the phone in both hands, as though that might help her sound less like a startled schoolgirl.

'You sound as though you were almost expecting me,' he remarked casually. 'Thank you for the print you sent me.'

'You liked it?' she asked nervously.

'I've seen worse,' he replied, a barely-perceptible hint of amusement lurking in his voice. 'The staff here inform me you haven't breakfasted yet. Will you join me?'

'Where are you?' she asked stupidly, blinking.

'Downstairs. In the foyer of this hotel,' he added, filling in her stunned silence. 'I'll see you in the breakfast-room. In ten minutes?' The line clicked dead in her ear.

Louise's heart was thudding as she twisted the taps in the bathroom closed, and scrambled into underwear and a deep yellow cotton dress that was all she could think of as suitable for breakfast with Bruno Xavier.

She wasn't sure whether the long, deep thrill inside her was delight or terror at the prospect of seeing him again. What had he come for, to praise her for the photograph—or to rip her apart?

She glossed her lips hurriedly in the mirror, wishing she was an exquisite platinum blonde with inch-long eyelashes. It had been romantically dark on the yacht. What would he think of her in the harsh light of day?

It was just under ten minutes later that she walked down the stairs, butterflies rising and settling in her stomach. A shaft of sunlight splashed on her as she walked into the little breakfast-room, making her dress blaze into a sunburst of summer gold for a second. He was sitting at the other end of the room, his chin resting on his clasped hands, and he watched her walk towards him for a long five seconds, his eyes unfathomable, before he rose to greet her.

'Did you sleep well?' he enquired, his height making him tower over her as he took her hand in a firm, brief handshake.

'Very well,' she answered, her throat feeling dry. The physical fact of his beauty had hit her like a hammer. He didn't look much like a playboy in the morning light. More, she thought ruefully, like some screen sex-symbol in those tight jeans and crisp cotton shirt. God, he was handsome! Her memory had blurred the perfect cut of those bronzed features, but the level stare of his storm-grey eyes was exactly as she knew it would be, an almost-physical shock all over again.

He assessed her calmly, doubling her sense of being badly off-balance.

'Yellow suits you very well,' he said gravely. 'It's the next best thing to wearing the sun.'

'Thank you,' she gulped. He eased her into her chair, and sat down opposite her.

'I had to come into Taormina to meet a business connection this morning, so I decided to have breakfast with you,' he informed her. 'Incidentally, I've taken the liberty of ordering it already. You don't mind?'

'N—no,' she said, drumming nervously on the snowy linen.

He smiled. 'I hope I didn't get you out of bed?'

'No, I was up.' She mustered her courage, and looked into his lazy, amused eyes. 'That photograph—did you like it?'

'"The real Bruno Xavier",' he murmured. 'They say I'm arrogant and conceited. Why shouldn't I like a highly flattering portrait of myself?'

The waiter brought them each a bowl of segmented citrus fruits sprinkled with Madeira sugar, and they started on the deliciously cool dish.

'Then what made you come out to see me this morning?' she demanded. His dark eyebrows climbed.

'To find out all about you, of course. Who you are, what you're like, where you come from—that sort of thing.' He spooned up some fruit, and glanced at her frozen expression. 'Why not? A model ought to know something about his artist, not so?'

She pushed her plate away, her appetite extinguished. His interest in her was more than a little overwhelming.

'Oh,' she said in a small voice.

'For example,' he went on, dabbing his mouth with a napkin, 'your first name.'

She looked down at her plate. 'It's—er—Louise.'

'Louise.' The name fitted perfectly on that sexy mouth. 'An unusual choice for an Englishwoman.'

'My father's name was Louis,' she told him. She drew another deep breath; the sensation of being without oxygen seemed to be a part of his effect on her.

'*Was?*' he repeated quietly.

'He died some years ago.' She barely noticed the waiter replacing her untouched fruit-salad with bacon and eggs. 'I'm sure you're going to find me extremely dull, Signore Xavier——'

'On the contrary,' he interrupted calmly, 'I'm finding you extremely interesting. I'm sorry to hear about your father. An accident?'

'No—he died of leukaemia.'

The bronzed face opposite her was serious now, his eyes gentle on hers. 'I'm sorry again. Leukaemia's a tragic disease. Was it chronic or acute?'

'Chronic,' she answered, slightly surprised. 'Do you know something about it?'

'A cousin of my own age died of acute leukaemia when I was a boy. I've never forgotten the loss.' He turned back to his breakfast. 'Who interested you in photography, then, Louise Jordan—your father?'

'Yes.' Her initial shock was thawing slightly now, but the excitement of his presence still wasn't allowing her to eat, and she stared into the twin yellow eyes of her fried eggs blankly. 'He was a very gifted amateur.' She lapsed into silence, feeling absurdly clumsy in the face of his dangerously magnetic elegance.

Bruno Xavier leaned back in his chair, sipped at his black coffee, and glanced at her coolly over the cup.

'You're not very forthcoming,' he remarked. 'You weren't so shy when we first met. What else do I know about you? Let me see. Occupation—photojournalist, of course. Place of birth—Erith, Kent. Born June 23—that makes you Cancer, *n'est ce pas?* Very feminine, but apt to be reserved. Place of residence, England. Height, 1 metre 68 centimetres. Have I left anything out? Ah yes, of course.' His eyes danced wickedly as he smiled, showing beautiful white teeth. 'I forgot distinguishing marks: a birthmark on the inside of the right thigh. Which sounds absolutely delicious, if I may say so.'

'You've been looking at my passport!' Louise gasped, remembering that she'd had to leave it with reception.

'I was intrigued by you, Miss Jordan,' he confessed mildly. 'And the manager was very obliging.' For a second, outrage struggled with amusement inside her. And then she couldn't stop the wry smile that curved across her mouth. Wicked as he was, the man's charm was very potent.

'Of course the manager would be obliging for Bruno Xavier,' she said with a touch of dryness. 'Do you always get exactly what you want?'

'No. More often I get what I deserve.' His mouth turned down in that hauntingly self-mocking way that had so intrigued her the night of the party. He glanced at her untouched plate. 'Don't you like your breakfast?'

'I'm not very hungry, signore,' she said. 'And you have a way of taking my appetite away!'

'Am I so horrifying?'

'Disturbing would be a better word,' she admitted.

His eyes sparkled with inner laughter. 'Ah—the difference between a hurricane and an earthquake. Which reminds me—I trust you weren't injured in yesterday's little performance?'

'No—I was in a restuarant at the time, as a matter of fact. It was rather strange——' She stopped, and he tilted his head enquiringly.

'What was strange?' Hesitantly, she told him about her muzzy feeling just before the quake. He heard her out in silence.

'So,' he said when she'd finished. 'You have the gift. It's very rare, Louise Jordan.'

'The gift?'

'The gift of foreseeing earthquakes. You could make a fortune renting yourself out to the Californians.' He was looking at her with thoughtful, smoky eyes. 'I've heard of this ability, but I thought it was restricted to gypsies and horses.'

'Which am I, then?' she smiled.

'A gypsy, to judge by those very lovely green eyes,' he remarked calmly. The compliment brought colour to her cheeks, but he didn't seem to notice. 'You shouldn't joke about it,' he went on quietly. 'It's a powerful thing you have there. If you ever get that feeling again, Louise Jordan, climb under the nearest table.'

'I'll try and remember,' she said, not sure whether he was teasing or not. He glanced at the slim gold watch on his wrist.

'I'm afraid I must keep an appointment in a few minutes,' he said regretfully. His eyes met hers with an almost shocking directness. 'I'm glad I came. I wanted very much to see whether you were as beautiful as I remembered.' His smile was sexy, warm. 'You're not. You're much more so. I was abstracted that night, thinking of other things.' She sat humbly, hypnotised by him, not daring to believe that the warmth and friendliness in him were real. 'And you have more than beauty. You have freshness and innocence, which are more important than anything else.'

She made a helpless little gesture. 'You hardly know me, signore——'

'Which is why we should get to know each other better,' he said gently. 'You agree?'

'I have very little to offer someone like you,' she said, searching carefully for the right words. Maybe he imagined her to be a lot more glamorous than she really was! 'We come from different worlds, signore. I'm an ordinary working girl, while you—you're someone special.'

'I hope not,' he smiled. 'It's nicer to be ordinary. Listen to me, Louise. I want to give you something in return for that portrait of me. A little thank you. I'm going to be scuba diving off Naxos tomorrow afternoon. You probably know that there are all sorts of traces of underwater volcanic eruptions there, including a network of caves. I want to take a closer look. Have you ever dived?'

'Only a few times, when I was a schoolgirl,' she said, shaking her glossy head. 'I've probably forgotten everything by now.'

'That's not serious. I could remind you of the basics in half-an-hour, and we'd be able to fit you out from *Merope*'s stores. Would you care to accompany me tomorrow? You could perhaps do some filming underwater, and tell your editor it's business.'

'I—I don't know what to say,' she hesitated awkwardly. God, what a perfect opportunity for an interview—but he'd never grant one, surely?

'You don't have to answer right now,' he smiled. 'Let me know by ship-to-shore if you decide to come. Even if you don't dive, the day will be rewarding.' He rose.

'Though I should warn you that if you won't come scuba diving with me, you will have to dine with me on *Merope* instead.'

'I'll ring you tonight,' she promised, still half disbelieving that this was all happening. He took her hand, and kissed the back of it gently. The warm touch of his mouth set gooseflesh rising all over her.

'*A bientôt*, then, Louise Jordan.' He picked up his blazer, smiled into her eyes, and walked out of the breakfast-room. She turned in her chair to stare after his tall figure.

Could all this really have followed on from one photograph taken on the darkened bridge of a yacht? It was the stuff of a play, a film—not Louise Jordan's workaday life!

The deep delight that was spreading steadily through her was suddenly checked at the memory of the telegram that was lying on her bedside table. *Damn!*

For the first time in two years, Louise found herself really hating her job. She stood up, and slowly walked back upstairs to her room. Instinctively she realised that she was facing a stark choice. Either to ask Bruno directly for an interview, risk a rebuff, and worst of all, jeopardise the friendship of the most marvellously warm and attractive man she'd ever met. Or to go diving with him, listen to everything he had to say, store it away in her brain—and write the article from memory.

And face the consequences later.

An ugly choice. She let her breath out with an explosive sigh. For the first time, she was coming up against the sordid realities of her chosen profession.

'*Journalists don't have friends.*' Hadn't that been the very first thing Percy had said to her, when she'd been a

fumbling cub reporter two years ago? She'd thought
that was just another cynical Widows comment at the
time.

Back in her room, she picked up Percy's telegram,
and considered. Bruno would certainly refuse if she
asked him for an interview. He might also become very
wary of her if he thought her 'fresh and innocent'
qualities were false. On the other hand, she would be
able to get that article painlessly, with a series of unique
photographs into the bargain, if she simply tagged
along and kept her eyes and ears open.

Visions of the complete lay-out flitted through her
mind—Bruno Xavier relaxing, that formidable mind
accessible and unguarded for once; big, glossy prints of
sunlit Italy to back up a series of stunning confidences
and revelations; a catalogue of private opinions on
every subject under the sun. And, she realised wryly,
photographs of that splendid body in a bathing
costume would be guaranteed to pull every female
reader from London to New York!

But what about her budding friendship with him—
she dared not call it romance——? When he read her
article, he'd explode, and it would explode with him.

Maybe, though, if the article were a very special one,
an article with the same profound, penetrating quality
of that portrait, it would be different?

The thought cheered her immensely. After all, she
wouldn't be going to write some cheap, inaccurate
story—the kind of mental burglary that the gossip
papers specialised in. She was going to write something
worthy of the man, a poetic and serious analysis of his
mind and heart.

It crossed her mind vaguely that it might be
presumptuous to think of writing something as

penetrating as that on such a short acquaintance, but she brushed the thought away. She had talent, didn't she? She'd done it with the camera—why not with the pen?

She jumped up, excitement rippling through her. Luck had delivered Bruno Xavier to her on a plate, and if she wrote this article, it could be the making of her career. Percy had been right—this was a fantastic opportunity for her.

She's never faced a challenge anything like this in two years; and succeeding in it would lift her straight out of the humdrum and into the élite. That magic group of journalists who commanded the most important interviews, the best salaries, the most interesting jobs. A very powerful incentive indeed. And as Sophie had pointed out, natural phenomena came and went. Unique people had classic human interest.

The idea was seeming less and less distasteful to her. After all, she told herself briskly, people in Bruno's position get completely inured to publicity! And there was good precedent for writers using friendships to create biographies—look at Boswell and Johnson. As for the budding romance idea—Bruno Xavier couldn't *possibly* give a damn about her. What was she kidding herself about? She wasn't risking anything. The most he'd have in mind would be getting her into bed.

Yes! She was going to do it, and the hell with the consequences! Bruno the hunter was about to become the hunted! She tugged off her yellow dress, deciding to have the bath that Bruno's arrival had interrupted.

Now, she wondered, where was she going to find an underwater housing for the Pentax? There must be plenty of specialist photographers' shops in Taormina. Should she risk taking a little notebook? Much too obvious. She'd have to think of something else. And what could she recall of the scuba-diving lessons they'd had at school one summer?

She peered out of her window at the white peak of Etna. Please, she begged the mountain, sister to sister—don't erupt until after tomorrow afternoon!

CHAPTER THREE

NAXOS shimmered white-hot in the noonday sun. Her bikini wasn't much protection against the hypnotic rays, but she was too contented and hot to think of putting her T-shirt back on. The beach scorched under Louise's towel, and the sea was a deliciously inviting cool turquoise. Clear as glass, she thought longingly. It was going to be so good to get under that cool translucency. Her skin was slippery with heat, and her sunglasses slid down the rim of her petite nose as she looked up hopefully at the sound of a motorboat. He was due to meet her here in a few minutes, and she was conscious of a slight ache of anticipation. Over the ship-to-shore telephone that husky voice with its fascinating accent had been friendly, even warm. It wasn't until she'd actually replaced the receiver that she realised how much she was looking forward to meeting him again . . .

The beautiful beach was almost empty, everyone having retired for lunch, leaving the golden-white sand to the sun-addicts and to her. Her inevitable bulky bag was beside her. Lorenzo Sanstefano in Taormina had rented her a special waterproof housing for her Pentax. She'd never used one before, and had been rehearsing carefully in the bath that morning, learning to use the knurled plastic knobs that operated the camera's controls from the outside. She'd decided in advance to use a 35mm lens, just wide enough to be useful for any underwater scene without distortion.

She'd used up some more of her expense account to buy another piece of equipment which wouldn't be going underwater—a Sony micro-recorder.

The little machine had given her more qualms than anything else. She'd been captivated by the ingenuity of the miniature silver device; no bigger than a packet of cigarettes, it took tiny cassettes smaller than a thin matchbox. She could unobtrusively switch it on at any time, and record any conversation with no one knowing a thing. Yet the micro-recorder somehow made what she was doing seem all the more unfair. Having it made her feel unpleasantly like a spy, a sneak. She'd struggled to fight the guilty feeling down, telling herself that she was just being practical in using it, but the temptation to leave it behind had been very strong that morning.

The fact remained, however, that without it she'd have only her memory to rely on. With it, she'd be able to have a perfect record of anything interesting Bruno might say, without inaccuracies or omissions. And in the end, she'd convinced herself that using it was actually fairer on Bruno—at least this way she could be certain that she wasn't going to mis-report him. So the recorder had been included, and was accessibly tucked in among her clothes in the bag.

Feeling rather like a recently-outfitted female James Bond, she drew her brown knees up to her breast, and clasped her arms round them. Her broad straw hat cast a speckled shade over her face and shoulders. She was excited about the afternoon; excited at the prospect of being with him again, of maybe getting the most important interview of her career. Excited at the thought of doing things with him, learning about him . . .

A slim white motor-launch was approaching, and

with a tingle of nerves. Louise stood up to wave, sure that it would be Bruno. It was. She made out his tall figure at the wheel, accompanied by a middle-aged crew-member from *Merope*. Smiling, she walked down to the water's edge to meet them, a slim golden figure with the breeze tossing her dark hair.

'Have you been waiting long?' he called, guiding the launch slowly through the shallows.

'Only a few minutes.' He was wearing tattered denim shorts and a white T-shirt that clung to his magnificent torso. The casual clothes gave him the seductively wild look of a millionaire beach-boy; but that unforgettable tanned face was too authoritative, too masterful for the delusion to fool Louise. He looked superb to her, utterly male, utterly free. His salt-stiffened dark hair told her he'd already been in the sea today.

'I don't want to beach the launch. Can you wade out to us?'

She nodded, hoisting her bag high, and waded through the cool water to the launch. It was bigger than she'd expected, and the twin motors in the stern looked venomously powerful. She passed her bag to Bruno, tossed her hat into the launch, and reached slender golden fingers up to his so-much-bigger bronze hands, to be hauled upwards with no more effort than if she'd been a salmon.

'Welcome aboard.' She smiled up into the real welcome that sparkled in his eyes, her heart tight with the pleasure of seeing him. Was this the formidable Bruno Xavier, man of iron? In the sunlight he was younger than she'd remembered, the hard aggression in his poise more challenging. There would be no melancholy today, that was certain. She stumbled lightly against the side, and the arms he steadied her with were hard, but sun-warm under her fingers. 'You'll be a sailor before long,' he smiled, straightening her. His eyes dropped to take in her figure with calm interest. They were amethyst-tinted this afternoon, ruthlessly self confident as he noted the fine satin of her skin, the modest black nylon of her bikini. She stooped, flushing slightly, and tugged out her towel to dry her wet legs. 'This is Beppo,' he said, introducing her to the grinning crewman. 'He knows more about this coast than anyone.'

'*Al vostro servizio*,' Beppo bowed with old-fashioned grace, and smiled at his master. Old friends, she guessed instinctively; whatever else he became, Bruno would always command the respect of men like this, men of the people. The aft of the launch was neatly stacked with diving-gear—oxygen cylinders, rubber suits, masks, weighted belts. Leaving her to find a seat, Bruno picked his way to the wheel. 'We'll be diving just out there,' he told her, pointing out to where the turquoise of the sea became cobalt, indicating deeper water. He smiled up at the distant peak of Etna. 'Your subject seems camera-shy, no?' The engines exploded into thrusting life, and she clung to the seat as he spun the launch in a tight curve, and accelerated out to sea. Beppo passed her a cushion with a friendly nod, and she tucked it gratefully behind her back.

Like *Merope* herself, the launch was spotless, and the gear in the stern was all superb-quality equipment—though well-used to judge by the loved and cared-for look of the stuff. He caught her green eyes studying the equipment over the rim of her sunglasses, and smiled.

'Worried?'

'Just hoping I'll be all right!' She had warned him yesterday that she wasn't an expert diver.

'I'll take care of you,' he promised. And the arms that rested on the slim steel wheel did look reassuringly muscular and protective, she had to admit. It was a glossy picture from some Sunday Magazine advertisement, Louise thought; the rakish white launch scything through the sunlit water, impeccably blue sky above, jewel-bright Mediterranean below. So this was how the rich amused themselves? He had everything, she realised with a touch of awe. Looks, physique, wealth, taste . . . This wasn't the heavy-handed striving after trendiness she'd seen in so many of her friends; Bruno Xavier had unmistakably *arrived*. A man who knew what he wanted, who didn't build cages to imprison himself in.

About two hundred yards out to sea, where the green tint of the water abruptly changed to royal blue, he shut off the throttle, and helped Beppo unship the cast-iron anchor. It plummeted down through the clear water, visible even on the shingled bottom deep below.

'We'll start from here,' he decided. 'The caves begin just against the reef, not more than twenty feet down.' As if sensing her sudden twist of nerves, he held her eyes. 'Just relax. I'm going to show you how the gear works, and I want you to listen very carefully. It's not difficult, but it is important.' She sat watching intently as he explained the valves and masks, trying to remember everything, and trying to listen to his concise words, rather than to that bewitching accent. She must find out where he'd been born, where his childhood had been . . .

'Shall I say it all again?' he enquired, his tanned face calm.

'No—I think I've got it.' She drew a breath that was anxious enough to make Beppo chuckle. Bruno nodded, and studied her figure with tranquil frankness.

'The suit ought to fit you well.' With unhurried deftness, he began to sort the gear into two groups. 'We won't bother with full suits, because it's not winter. But it's surprisingly cold down there, even in July, so wet-suits are important. Okay?'

'Okay,' she nodded, realising that he was reassuring her, and feeling a glow of gratitude at his perception of her nervousness.

'We're going to kit you out first, Louise. We start with the suit.' She stepped gingerly into the wet-suit he held out for her, her skin brushing shiveringly against his. Like a one-piece costume, except that it came up to her throat and was secured with a long zip from throat to abdomen, it was made of a thick, flexible rubber. Once submerged, water would creep beneath it, and become warmed by her own body, providing an insulating layer against the cold. A broad vertical yellow stripe down the matte black front was designed for easy recognition. It felt close and snug over her bikini, and she tugged her chestnut hair out of the back, feeling marginally more secure. He watched as she tied the heavy tresses into a ponytail, then passed her the flippers. Thick rubber anklets helped secure these against accidents.

'Sit,' he commanded. They looped the oxygen cylinders over her shoulders, and tugged the webbing straps tight. The equipment was uncomfortably heavy, adding to her anxiety even though she knew that underwater she'd scarcely be aware of the life-giving tanks on her back. He made her test the full-face mask, drawing the pure oxygen into her lungs, until she'd regulated the valve to her satisfaction.

Hands on hips, he smiled down at her. 'You look very professional. Still nervous?'

Louise took the mask off, faintly tasting metal and rubber. 'Not too bad,' she said in a small voice. His mouth curved into a smile, and he cupped her chin in warm fingers. 'Don't be such a bundle of nerves. You'll feel a lot better once we're under.'

'I'll try to relax,' she said, resisting the urge to rub her cheek against his hand like a cat.

'Good. Get your camera ready in the meantime.' She sat with the Pentax in her lap, covertly watching the economical efficiency with which he prepared.

He didn't have a playboy's figure. He was hard and lithely muscular, so little spare flesh on his bronzed body that every muscle was momentarily defined as he moved. No pampered house-cat, but a big, dangerously hungry tiger whose claws just happened temporarily to be sheathed. Her throat felt oddly constricted, and she dropped her eyes confusedly from the intriguing black triangle of his costume. A big, hungry tiger with a big, hungry ego; he was profoundly, almost primitively masculine, his skin crackling with life from the dark curls down his stomach to the ripple of deep-stirring muscle in his thighs. Seeing his near-naked body like this somehow helped her understand the fierce drive in him to achieve, to win, to succeed. He was as much like other men as a ten-carat diamond is like pebbles. Her veiled green eyes were drawn irresistibly to the tautening of his powerful stomach muscles as he hauled his own wet-suit on. It fitted his lean waist and flanks like a glove, a red recognition strip across the broad swell of his shoulders. Beppo heaved the oxygen tanks on to his back, and he tugged the straps taut across stomach and chest before putting on the flippers. He smiled at her. 'Ready?'

'Ready,' she nodded, fighting down butterflies of

anxiety and excitement. He rinsed the glass of their masks in the water, and handed her her own. Her fingers were unsteady as she pulled it over her face, feeling the trickle of cold water against her sun-warmed skin. It covered her whole face, the oxygen-tube built into it so she could breathe normally. Beppo patted her shoulder comfortingly, and fastened the weight-belt around her slender waist. The extra pounds, designed to keep her buoyancy neutral underwater, weighted her down even further. Through the wide glass window, she looked imploringly at Bruno. His grin was a flash of white.

'The best thing is to get under at once. Do exactly as I do.' He sat on the gunwale, slipped the mask over his face, and pulled it tight. Then, holding it firmly with one hand, toppled backwards into the water and vanished with barely a splash.

Feminine terror, held down while he was there so big and reassuring, rose up in her. Beppo placed her camera into her unsteady fingers. His hands were soothing on her shoulders, as though he were gentling a nervy horse. He put her own hand on to her mask, and tipped her smoothly backwards. The world turned upside down,- and she splashed into the water, sinking with shut eyes. As the water closed over her head, an irrational panic told her she couldn't breathe, she'd *drown*, and she thrashed her way upwards blindly. Strong arms slid round her waist, immobilising her, and from nowhere Bruno drew her against the hard comfort of his body. She sucked in air with a long shudder.

Deliciously pure oxygen, and not strangling water, hissed into her lungs, and she went limp in a reaction of sheer relief. She opened her eyes languidly, holding on round Bruno's neck. Through the glass of his mask he smiled, and raised dark eyebrows in a silent question, *Okay?*

She nodded, feeling like a fool. The silence was infinite, and the first cool creeping-in of water over her skin was refreshing under the suit. He pointed upwards. The surface was an undulating sheet of silvery brightness, the launch a long, shark-like shape an amazingly long way above them.

He let her slide away from him, and jack-knifed his powerful body to swim downwards. Hesitantly, she followed. The world was blue, a deep, heavenly blue that shimmered with the filtered sunlight from high above. The bottom below was a waving field of sea-grass, interspersed with stretches of blue-gold sand. A shoal of glinting fish shimmered past Bruno as he kicked steadily downwards. The beauty of it all melted her terror as though it had never existed. Weightless, she followed . . .

The late afternoon sunlight was honey over her cool skin. She sipped the rough, fragrant red wine, feeling as though every sinew in her body had been stretched and toned. The little trattoria was quiet, and the few patrons seemed not to have noticed that the big man sitting by the window with the green-eyed brunette was Bruno Xavier.

Outside, the beach stretched away in a golden haze. Beppo was dozing in the launch with a bottle of chianti at his side, the diving gear neatly stacked away.

'That was an unforgettable experience,' she said quietly. 'I don't even know how to thank you, Signor Xavier.'

'You don't have to thank me. And my name is Bruno.' The wine glinted ruby as he drank. 'I hope the photographs make it all worthwhile for you.'

Worthwhile? It had been as beautiful as a dream—the slow ballet of underwater movement, the honeycomb of volcanic caves that ran deep blue and infinitely mysterious under Naxos, probably to the molten core of Etna itself; the presence of Bruno beside her, his powerful body as adapted to the water as a dolphin's. What she'd said had been the truth. She'd never forget the beauty he'd shown her, the wonders they'd shared. She'd used up three rolls of film, recording that exquisitely silent undersea kingdom, the caves and the turquoise canyons. In the sunlight, after the dive, she'd taken a succession of portraits of Bruno, trying to capture the lithe spontanaeity of his movements, the way the sun blazed off the living bronze statue of his magnificent body. But no photographs, she knew, would ever completely capture the magic of this afternoon. Or the magic of now, when his mood was so captivatingly gentle that she yearned for him . . .

'You chose a wonderful way of thanking me for a very unworthy gift,' she said. 'I didn't deserve all this.'

'I didn't mean to thank you simply for the picture,' he said with a smile. 'That would have been vanity, no?'

'Then why?'

'That's a little hard to answer.' He drank slowly, thick lashes veiling his eyes. She felt a strange little tug of jealousy for the rim of the glass, so intimate against that sensual mouth. 'Maybe just for seeing me in a particular way,' he said, cradling the glass in both hands. 'I no longer look at pictures of myself, Louise. Maybe that sounds melodramatic? After ten years of high-level exposure, though, my own image bores me. Does that make sense to you?' She nodded, thinking that his velvet voice was as physical a pleasure as nestling in a bearskin rug. 'Everywhere I go, lenses stare at me, microphones appear under my nose, questions, demands, importunate enquiries. There've been moments when I was on the brink of smashing out at them all, tearing a pathway through.' The tiger was suddenly visible in him, in the pagan fury of his eyes, the split second's unleashing of muscle under his casual clothes. Then visibly willing his body to relax, he grimaced. 'It would become intolerable if I didn't have the ability to retire behind a wall.'

She nodded, her eyes caressing his face, so darkly virile with its high cheekbones and carved mouth. His mention of microphones reminded her of the Sony in her own bag, just beside her. Unobtrusively, she reached down and found its smooth shape among her clothes and hairbrushes. She pressed the record button, making sure that the microphone grille wasn't covered, and rested her chin in her hands. If her memory missed out any details, she could at least have a record of what he'd said.

'And my portrait was special?' she smiled.

'In a way. You made me look rather cynical, rather old,' he admitted ruefully. She smiled. The cynicism she'd noticed in him that first night had been almost non-existent today. And although the leashed power in him was always perceptible, a hint of danger beneath the surface, it was as though her company somehow gentled him, allowing him to shed the sardonic mask which was probably so much a part of his defences. 'I'm thirty-six,' he acknowledged, 'and sometimes that feels like an eternity. But you got past my wall somehow. You made me look human—not just a clichéd image. As though you could see how I felt, and sympathised. That was something special. And for that,' he said softly, 'I'm grateful, Louise Jordan.'

His tone made her heart suddenly lurch inside her, and she could no more have looked away from those compelling eyes than a butterfly could have escaped from its pin. For the first time, it occurred to her that she might be out of her depth with this man. A long, long way out.

'*Di niente*,' she said, trying hard to sound playful. She'd more than once sensed the latent passion in him, and for all his present gentle, almost tender mood, she would never dare stir that half-asleep tiger in any way; what if he really desired her, the way those magnificent eyes had smokily hinted? What if he made even a casual effort to seduce her?

With another stomach-churning realisation, she knew that Bruno Xavier's loving wouldn't be the fumbling affair of the other men she'd known. In fact, the thought of her own possible reaction to him was almost too frightening to contemplate. She didn't want to think of what would happen to her, of the way his touch would change the assumptions she'd always had about men and love and sex. Maybe the whole cool, nonchalant structure of her world would simply crumple, leaving her utterly naked. More likely, it would go up in one sheet of flame, scorching the butterfly inside!

With the alarming sense that she had been dancing blithely along the edge of a precipice, Louise tried to jerk herself into mental awareness. It was one thing to dream hazily about Bruno Xavier. Quite another to face those living eyes across a table in a seaside village trattoria, and feel the first bone-melting hints of his desire for her.

'Bruno——' His name was like brandy on her tongue, the first time she'd ever used it.

'Hmmm?'

'I——' She bit her satiny lip. Should she tell him about the microphone? If there was any real feeling growing between them, shouldn't she warn him? She stared mistily into his eyes. Would he be angry? Alternatives danced restlessly in her mind. She wanted that article. Would he let her interview him, though? If she was to tell Bruno about the tape-recorder, it must be now——

'What is it, little one?' He reached out, and took her own hand in long, strong fingers. 'There's suddenly a shadow in those witching eyes. What's on your mind?'

'Just a shadow, like you said.' She smiled uncertainly, doubt twisting in her mind.

'You're too young to even know what a shadow is,' he smiled, caressing the sensitive back of her hand softly. Gooseflesh stirred all over her body, and with a helpless little sound in her throat, she felt that moment recede for ever. She couldn't tell him now about the article she was planning ... 'Cinnamon silk,' he said gently, studying her skin with smoky eyes. 'I thought the English were supposed to be pale and sunless?'

'They are,' she smiled timidly.

'You must have gypsy blood, then. You have a gypsy's eyes, Louise, and the gypsy gift of foretelling earthquakes. When exposed to the sun, the English blister and peel like delicate paint. Your skin drinks up the sun, and turns it into wild honey.' Dazzled by his smile, she could only shake her head mutely. 'Perhaps you're the Golden Bee herself?'

'Who's the Golden Bee?' she asked.

'It's an ancient Mediterranean legend,' he said. 'They say that the sun is a flower, and that only one magic bee knows the secret of gathering his nectar. She is called

the Golden Bee, because the honey she makes is gold.'
He smiled. 'You must be starving, little bee. Shall I
order something to eat?'

'I couldn't get a morsel down,' she said truthfully. He
had put a lump in her throat that barely let her breathe.

'Naxos wine is strong,' he warned. 'It comes from the
vineyards of Etna. I don't want to have to carry you
back to Taormina. Best eat something.' He summoned
the waiter with a nod, and ordered in rapid Italian.

'Bruno,' she said quietly when the waiter had gone, 'I
don't know why you're being so kind to me. I'm
nothing to you, just some journalist who took a
sympathetic picture of you. Why do you bother?'

'*Semplicitá*,' he said gently.

'What does that mean?' she pleaded.

'A very rare quality. Something like simplicity.
Purity, if you like.' He brushed his thumb across the
gentle swell of her mouth, and she closed her eyes
helplessly.

'You may be deceived in me,' she whispered, lifting
heavy lashes slowly.

'With those eyes? I don't think so. *Se pure mi dici 'na
bugia, é ingenua e santa, come la veritá.*'

' My Italian isn't very good,' she said with a tiny smile.

'It's a line from an old Neapolitan song. "Even if you
were to tell me a lie, it would be innocent and blessed as
the truth." '

'That's an incredible thing to say about anyone,' she
said, thinking dazedly, guiltily of the tape-recorder
whirring silently in her bag. 'You mustn't!'

'It's the penalty of the kind of life I lead,' he smiled,
beautiful white teeth glinting against his bronzed face.
'Ninety-nine percent of the time I'm pathologically
suspicious. The other one percent of the time, I'm

totally trusting.' He leaned back, and considered her with amused, sexily narrowed eyes. 'Now and then everyone's allowed to break out and go a little crazy, no?'

'But how do you know you can trust me?'

'I don't know,' he shrugged. 'I just do.'

'A most un-millionaire-like statement,' she said, shaking her glossy head slowly.

He threw back his head and laughed with pure delight. 'I wasn't always a millionaire, honey bee. Once upon a time I went barefoot because I didn't even have a pair of shoes.'

'Where was that?'

He looked at her assessingly. 'Ajaccio.'

'In Corsica?' He nodded. So *that* was why his accent was such a strange mixture of Italian and French inflections! 'I might have guessed that you'd share the same nationality as Napoleon,' she smiled. 'Were you so poor, then?'

'Illegitimacy brings many burdens,' he said softly, 'of which poverty is one of the least.' His pupils were dark and expanded, leaving merely a silver rim under long lashes.

'You were born out of marriage?' Fascinated, she studied that classically virile face. 'Who are your parents?'

'They're both dead now.' He toyed with the cheap wine-glass, its simple shape somehow suiting the uncompromising strength of his fingers. 'My mother was a simple peasant woman, Louise. Simple, and very beautiful. She lived on one of the ancient estates on the island, belonging to the noble French family of de Xavier.' He nodded at her flash of interest. 'Yes. I took my father's name. Or as much of it as I needed. The "de" didn't interest me—such things mean nothing to a man. But I wanted a name.' The dark candles that had suddenly been lit in his eyes dimmed. 'This is not something I ever talk about, *cara mia*. Why should I bore you?'

'Oh please,' she begged. 'Please—I'm fascinated!' The waiter materialised with a beaming smile and a great platter of *frutti di mare*—clams, shrimps, baby octopus fried in batter, succulent flakes of swordfish and tunny, the tiny local mussels called *vongole*, all mixed in a deliciously crisp pile with wafers of sweet Sicilian lemon. Her earlier loss of appetite forgotten, Louise let him pile her plate high, and ate with relish as she listened.

'Your father was a member of the aristocratic family?' she probed, her parted lips shining with butter-sauce.

'The only son.' A smile dry as the chianti crossed his mobile mouth. 'Etienne de Xavier. By all accounts a beautiful boy, spoiled and indulged by a doting mother to the extent that he'd become unmanageably wild. Not even the Baron could control him.'

' "By all accounts"?' she repeated.

'I never knew him. He and my mother had a brief, tempestuous affair which lasted barely six months, and ended as all such liaisons must—with the girl's pregnancy, and the man's abrupt departure. Forced, I need not add, by his indignant father. The Baron sent his son off to Paris to forget the whole thing. A precautionary measure,' he added, a saturnine gleam in his eyes. 'for there were those among my mother's relatives not above settling such a matter of honour in the usual Corsican manner. With a knife on a moonless night.'

She shuddered, tilting her glossy head to one side,

and searching his face with dark-fringed eyes as clear as rock-pools. 'And your mother?'

'The Baron offered to find her a place somewhere in Italy. A convent, you understand, where she could live out her pregnancy peacefully—and discreetly—and leave the child to the care of the nuns afterwards. Do not offend our host by neglecting the *frutti di mare*,' he advised, selecting a crisp pink shrimp and popping it into her mouth. He watched her, smiling with a faint touch of irony as she ate, oblivious, wide-eyed and eager for the story to continue. 'My mother was too proud for that. Besides, she had, I believe, truly loved Etienne, scapegrace though he was. She wanted his child. So she insisted on remaining exactly where she was, and continuing her life exactly as before. This the Baron found intolerable, of course. He was a fierce old man who was obsessed with the family name above all else.'

'So what happened?' she demanded breathlessly.

Bruno rinsed his mouth out with wine, and gulped it down. His face was harsher now, his mouth bitter, as though the wine had been vinegar. 'Etienne's trip to Paris, in the meantime, proved his last escapade, *mia cara* Louise. He lived like a Prince for six weeks, drove his sports car into the Seine one night after a party and was drowned.' She froze, graceful fingers dripping lemon-juice.

'And your mother?'

He shook his head staring back into the past. 'I don't think she was really alive after that. She had lived, always, in hope of his return.' He saw the sudden glistening of her eyes, and reached out to touch her cheek. 'Have some more wine, little bee—it will take that melancholy out of those emeralds.'

'I can't help it—it's so sad!'

'It was certainly sad for my mother,' he said drily. 'She had defied the Baron in not leaving Corsica, and he retaliated by dismissing her from his estate. She had to leave the cottage where she was born, and find other work, heavy as she was. There was precious little work for her to do in Ajaccio, especially after my birth. Poverty and disgrace are terrible things, far worse with an infant son to care for. And Etienne's death took the light from her eyes. We left Ajaccio, and did what the Corsicans have always done in times of trouble—made for the high ground.' He twisted a heavy gold ring on his finger. She hadn't noticed it before, an antique-looking signet with a falcon carved on the bezel. 'For three or four years we lived up in the mountains—which was how I came to take my first steps barefoot. As I say, she wasn't truly in this world any more, and I remember her as a silent, still woman, who would suddenly embrace me, and hold me close enough to hurt—never for any reason I could tell. She died when I was less than five, and I was taken in by distant relations in the town, who brought me up according to their own creed and experience.'

'Where they kind to you?' she asked softly.

'Considering that I was the illegitimate brat of a distant relative, and didn't even have a surname—yes, they were not unkind. I spent most of my childhood believing that my father had drowned at sea. But when I was twelve, one of my step-uncles told me the whole story of my birth.'

She watched the dark throat ripple as he drained his glass.

'What did you do?' she asked, almost dreading the answer.

'I thought for two days,' he smiled, 'and eventually

decided that I ought to kill the old Baron. It seemed to me, with my childish eyes, that my aristocratic grandfather was the true villain of the piece.'

'God,' she breathed.

'Don't look so horrified,' he said calmly. 'I didn't succeed, of course. But I did go and see Baron Philippe de Xavier in the end. He knew who I was at once, by my resemblance to *le pauvre Etienne*.'

'And?'

'I made some childish speech, accusing him of having destroyed both my mother and my father. He, by then, was a lonely old man. His own wife, who had been many years younger than he, was now dead—and he faced nothing but a disconsolate old age, and the extinction of a family name which had lasted since Roman times.' Studying his hands with hooded eyes, Bruno fell silent.

'Did he take you in?' she asked, watching the sunset gild the harsh, beautiful lines of his face.

'Yes,' he said, looking up with the dying sun in his eyes. 'He became my grandfather in deed as well as in name—partly, I think, out of some obscure remorse at the way things had turned out, and partly so that the family name shouldn't die out. He insisted on a grandpaternal adoption proceeding, and wanted me to take the de Xavier name.' Again that scimitar-blade smile. 'Xavier was enough for me. It was a more democratic age, anyway. It was time to let the "de" fade into the past.'

'It's an unbelievable story,' she said, her voice shaking slightly. Her slender brows curved down over her eyes as she tried to visualise the fierce child he had once been, the strange, harsh experiences that had shaped his life.

'It's not a story I've told to a living soul in full,' he said, grey eyes shot with smiling flame. 'Have I entertained you?'

'You've bewitched me,' she said quietly. 'What happened then?'

'My grandfather and I lived together for some years,' he shrugged. 'In a belated excess of family feeling, he had me sent to the best schools he could find. What were in his opinion, at least, the best schools. I had the education of a nineteenth century French aristocrat, Louise. I learned to fence like an Italian, ride like a German, speak like a Frenchman. Useless, expensive, pleasurable things,' he smiled. 'I didn't really start to learn about the world until I left Corsica, and began to make my own way in the world.'

'After your Grandfather died?'

'Yes. He left the de Xavier estate to me in his will, of course—a crumbling *château* and a few hundred acres of wild, fertile, neglected Corsican hillside.'

'Didn't you want it?' she marvelled.

'I haven't been back for——' He thought. 'Six, seven years. The last time I saw *Le Faucon*, the sky was visible through the roof-beams, and the rose-garden had grown into a perfumed tangle of thorns. Only the wind and the ravens have it now.'

'It sounds weirdly beautiful,' she shuddered, dark lashes narrowed as she imagined the desolate place.

'It is. The most beautiful house on earth. You can see the coast of Spain across the sea on a good day, and to the north, the Côte d'Azure.' He smiled enigmatically at her. 'Even before I learned about Etienne, I thought that *Le Faucon* was the most desirable, most beautiful place in the world. I dreamed my childhood away on it.'

'But——' Incomprehension dimmed her emerald eyes. 'Why don't you go back, rebuild it?'

'I will. One day. When one woman manages to still the restlessness in me, when she tells me that my child is in her womb—then I will return to *Le Faucon*, and turn it into a palace. And put down roots, for ever. Until then—I live in yachts and expensive apartments, and amuse myself with work, money, parties——'

'And beautiful women,' she finished for him.

'And beautiful women,' he nodded. 'Am I so notorious?'

'You have a certain reputation,' she told him wryly, reflecting that there must be women ready to commit murder in the name of Bruno Xavier. 'It's easy to see that women find you—irresistible.'

'Really?' he purred, mock-solemn. 'And you, Louise Jordan—how do you find me?'

'Disturbing,' she admitted quietly.

'Yes.' He searched her face with suddenly intense grey eyes. 'Exactly as I find you, Louise Jordan.' She couldn't stop the shiver that crawled from her scalp down her back at his words. And, as on the night of the party, when he'd stared down her lens, those dark pupils seemed to be reaching into her very soul, a contact that was almost frighteningly intimate.

Then, coolly, he turned in his chair, and stared into the violet East, where the tranquil cone stood unmoved.

'And Etna has still not erupted.' He swung back, consulting the Rolex on his wrist, then hauled his windcheater off the chair. 'I want to see you again. Soon.'

'Are you going?' she asked with a sharp pang.

'I'm afraid that I must. I've already deferred the evening's business by an hour for the sake of your delicious eyes.'

'The evening's business—a woman?' she asked sweetly.

'Nothing so amusing,' he said with a rumble of laughter. 'Merely money. For the time being, *Merope* is my headquarters, and I have to receive an important business contact on board tonight.'

'I thought this was your holiday?' she said, rising with him in painful bewilderment at the end of this sunset dream.

'It is, little Louise. But I have too many responsibilities to ever be completely indifferent to the hours—no matter how sweetly they are spent.' His smile was a caress so intimate and gentle that she couldn't, just couldn't believe this was a sexy man's ordinary flirting. She stood in silence as he paid the bill, and then walked with him into the glory of the sunset outside. 'I'll take you to Mazzaró in the launch, and arrange a taxi from there up to Taormina. *Va bene?*' Her skin was cool against his as he linked arms with her on the walk to the launch. Within, though, she was a melting-pot of emotions—among which wonder was uppermost. Wonder that he should spend so much of his precious time on her. Wonder that there should be real affection in those dazzling eyes . . .

'*Va bene,*' she agreed. 'But only if on the way you'll continue your story just a little.'

'How far is a little?' he teased.

'Your first million.'

'You call that a little?' he said, arching dark eyebrows. 'Ah, *santa semplicitá* . . .

'. . . *a disconsolate old age, and the extinction of a family name which had lasted since Roman times.*' The tiny cassette turned steadily in the silver machine, the velvety voice with its intriguing inflection faithfully recorded on the unspooling ribbon, filling the quiet hotel room.

Three a.m. Coffee-cups and half-eaten sandwiches at the bedside, the shutters thrown wide to the cool of the Sicilian night. Cross-legged on her bed, paper and notes scattered all around her, Louise reached for the stop button, and shut off Bruno's voice for a moment. In the pool of light from her lamp, she was near-naked for the heat, only her silk bra and briefs making a concession to modesty.

Her pen raced across the pad, her full mouth twisted with concentration. The effort of writing and the tropical warmth of the night had lain a sheen across her satiny skin, dewing her face and arms; mingling with the langourous sweetness of Opium, she could smell the faint musk of her own sweat and the sea-salt of the afternoon's dive. She hadn't even stopped to bath after the taxi had dropped her off—it didn't matter. There would be time to bath when the story was on its way to London.

And what a spellbinding story it was, full of drama and passion, lit somehow with a stark Mediterranean light . . .

'His voice gives nothing away,' she wrote, her untidy writing racing across the paper, 'it is soft, always bewitchingly mellow. But his eyes tell the inner story; the colour in them shifts and changes as he speaks, like sunlight through clouds over deep water. When he speaks about Philippe de Xavier, those eyes are strange, ironic. There is a respect in them, maybe even a kind of love, for the fierce old man who destroyed so much happiness; but there is also a wry, profound regret for the folly of human nature, the waste that lies in such inevitable tragedies of love, and pride, and arrogant human will.

' "He became my grandfather," Bruno Xavier recounts, "in deed as well as in name—partly, I think, out of some obscure remorse ..." '

She was exhausted, yet driven on by a kind of demon now that the article was nearly complete. There were clumsy sentences here and there, passages which could have done with polishing, but she wasn't going to spend the time that needed. Deep in her gut, she knew that this was the most powerful article she'd ever written—a mixture of in-depth interview and biographical story that somehow managed to capture something of Bruno Xavier's mind and heart. Thank God she'd used the micro-recorder. Without it, she'd have been utterly lost.

She had written of him as she saw him, leaving out none of the insights she'd had, sparing nothing. She hadn't even bothered to disguise the fact that Bruno stirred her in the most powerful way, that she was close to adoration in her attitude to him. That was incidental—what mattered was getting it all down, stamping the white paper indelibly with the brilliant colours of her impressions, the savage, pagan beauty of Bruno's soul. And somehow, in that near-impossible goal, she'd succeeded. He was there—proud, gentle, frightening—the complex, fascinating man she'd known for a bare few days, but would never forget.

She reached out, and gulped down the lukewarm remainder of her coffee, left outside her door by the night porter. The photographs would have to go to London undeveloped; there wasn't time to have Cervello print them in Catania. Percy would have to have them done at the office, and make his choice, probably while the presses were actually running. There was still time, just time, to get the story to *Woman Today* by the week-end. Etna was for the time being forgotten, pushed into the background by the infinitely more powerful and human story in the little silver machine.

She flicked on the recorder again, and listened intently, her green eyes smudged with tiredness now. She wrote again, her pen slurring across the paper. She was leaving out words here and there now—that didn't matter either. Percy would know what she meant . . .

Deep in the earth, a long shudder began, rattling the coffee-cups in their saucers. The hotel seemed to sway, ever so slightly, as the subterranean rumble swelled and faded in the silence of the night, like faraway thunder. She scrambled out of bed, and ran to the shutters. The red dot of Etna was unmoved, and the faint vibration under her feet faded into stillness. Not yet. The night was silent except for the bark of dogs, villages away. The tremor hadn't even shaken the sleepers out of their beds. Just another inch gone of the fuse that was burning towards the coming eruption. An omen? She waited for a few minutes, listening to the sounds of the night, but the earth was still, and she walked back to her bed. There were things more important than Etna on her mind now.

Dawn came cool and blue, with a music of blackbirds. In her tiny bathroom, she sluiced water over her face, and held a sopping face-cloth to her aching forehead. It was finished, almost ten thousand words of lyrical, passionate prose scattered on her unmade bed.

Muzzily, she pulled on a frock, and tried to cover her exhaustion with make-up in the mirror. The courier was leaving on the seven-thirty flight, and she'd have to be in Catánia by then.

What gave her the right to do this? That haunting question had surfaced more than once in her mind, and she'd always thrust it away. She hadn't asked his permission to write this article; on the other hand, he hadn't actually forbidden her to write it, had he? Would he be angry with her when he saw what she'd done? 'But it's all true,' she whispered to herself. 'I've written of you as you are, my love. You can't be angry with me, you *can't* . . .'

The day porter had just come on duty by the time she walked out into the sunlit early morning, clutching the bulky envelope that contained her article. In the square she found an early-rising taxi driver, and within fifteen minutes, was on the motorway to Catánia.

Tiredness had brought depression and anxiety, despite the brilliance of the day. She was convinced in her own mind that the article was a faithful portrait of Bruno. More—it was a sensitive analysis of the strange forces that had made him the way he was. But she couldn't ignore the grim shadow of his possible anger.

It would have been so simple to just pick up the telephone and ask him. But she didn't dare. She didn't dare contemplate the choice she would face if he forbade her to send it in. Could she just shelve what she had written at this stage, tear it up and never think of it again? Impossible. Her life-blood had gone into that story as much as his had. It *had* to be published.

Besides, she told herself firmly, she'd already made her decision. He'd known she was a journalist when he'd asked her to dive with him. He must have known, when he allowed her to photograph him, when he told her all the details about his boyhood, that he was giving her priceless material, material she couldn't possibly ignore. She fought back the uneasiness in her mind. To people in Bruno Xavier's position, publicity was inevitable. They barely noticed it.

And with luck, she told herself as the airport swung into view, he'd never even see the article.

CHAPTER FOUR

THE courier, portly and respectable in dark suit and greyhound badge, recognised Louise at once.

'For *Women Today* again?'

'Yes please—and it's terribly urgent.'

'I'll do my best.'

Feeling too exhausted to set off for Taormina yet, Louise made her way to the glassed-in coffee-bar that overlooked the tarmac, and found an empty table among the mêlée of departing and arriving passengers.

The *espresso* was fresh and strong, and she closed her eyes, slumping back in the plastic chair. The die was cast now. No returns, no second chances. There was no calling back that revealing, adoring article. Would he see the respect, the admiration that had inspired it? Or would that formidable temper snap when he saw what she'd done?

No choice but to wait and see.

She drank slowly. What had she achieved? Written the scoop story of her journalistic career. Given Percy an article and pictures he'd be able to syndicate across Britain. Earned enough money to buy herself a new set of cameras, or a very expensive diamond.

And betrayed the only man who'd ever set the blood racing through her veins.

No, she contradicted the thought sharply. It was no betrayal! She'd only done her job, only done what she was paid to do! Besides, it was also a question of art; she was a journalist, driven to write as some are driven

78

to paint or sing. She couldn't have stopped herself if she'd tried. She'd created something beautiful. She gulped down the scalding coffee. The passengers were walking in a long crocodile to the British Airways flight to Heathrow. Among them she recognised the portly, dapper shape of the courier. Her article was in that briefcase, on its way to Percy Widows.

Abruptly, the image of those wonderful grey eyes swam into her mind. He had trusted her! More—there had been tenderness in his eyes, tenderness in his touch. A bone-melting tenderness that might, miraculously, become something more ... But it can't be true, she told herself shakily, Bruno Xavier couldn't possibly be interested in a little journalist like me! He was only toying with me, the way he toys with all his women ...

No, her heart denied. It's you who've toyed with him. *You betrayed him.* A pain sharp as death lanced through her. All the half-suppressed doubts in her mind, all the reservations she'd managed to keep under a lid, began tumbling out in a horrific explosion of guilt. Dear God, what had possessed her? She must have been blind, her brain numbed by the Sicilian sun! She'd taken his confidence, and plastered it on every billboard. She stood up on shaky legs, and walked to the soundproof glass, as though somehow she could recall that dapper little figure, now at the base of the aluminium stairs that led up into the Trident. Her face was white, her conscience tearing away the mists of tiredness that had fuddled her brain. How in the name of all that was holy could she have done such a thing? As the depth of her own feelings became clearer, the full horror of the loss she'd risked was driven home in her heart. She hadn't just lost her integrity. She'd lost Bruno. Maybe for ever.

The heat-shimmer billowed around the great jet engines as they surged, and the Trident rolled forwards, beginning to pick up speed on the take-off runaway. A white spear, poised for a bitter wound.

She was biting her knuckles, though she didn't know it, her eyes pale as green ice.

Oh, sweet God, what had she done?

'I found it completely by accident,' Sophie explained taking the German-language magazine out of her bag and passing it over. 'How good is your German?'

'So-so,' Louise replied absently. She took the glossy magazine, and flipped through it carelessly. They were sitting in Aldo's, the little bar which the foreign journalists had by common consent made their evening rendezvous.

'The article's around page one hundred,' Sophie said. Louise nodded, other things on her mind. She had been longing to tell Sophie of her predicament, but hadn't been able to find the words. The photograph of Bruno jumped out of the glossy pages at her, and she paged back quickly. A sultry picture under a huge headline. He had been photographed sitting in some high-society restaurant with his tie tugged loose, the aggression in those smoky eyes undimmed by the near-empty bottle of Remy-Martin on the table. Or the very *décolleté* blonde nestling next to him, one beautiful hand spread possessively—and shamelessly high—on the inside of his thigh.

'That's the one,' Sophie nodded. 'Want me to translate?'

'No,' Louise said tensely. The writer's name had sent a cold chill through her. Laura Ackermann. She glanced at the date, saw it was last month, and ploughed into the German text. '*Xavier's bed,*' she translated for herself, *'was immense, a———'* She looked up at Sophie, pale-faced. 'What's a *Liebespalast*?'

Sophie shrugged. 'A palace of love.' She watched Louise's stunned expression. 'It's terrible, isn't it?'

Louise read on. Terrible wasn't the word. It was the most appalling piece of journalism she'd ever seen. Laura Ackermann, the blonde in the photograph, was evidently a regular contributor to the magazine. The gist of her story was crudely simple.

She claimed to have had a passionate affair with Bruno Xavier, on the basis of which she had written 'an authoritative account of his personality and lifestyle'. Which meant, Louise realised with flaming cheeks, a biologically uninhibited account of his lovemaking prowess and technique. She struggled with the unfamiliar words for two or three paragraphs, scarcely able to believe what she was reading. The woman's style didn't even rise to the level of eroticism—it was sheer, crude pornography, using Bruno's name and describing Laura's own ecstatic reactions in lurid terms.

Louise stared incredulously at the photograph again, then threw the magazine on to the table, too sickened to read any more.

'So *that's* what Percy was talking about,' she whispered, almost to herself. 'I feel ill!'

'The woman's a tart,' Sophie agreed, turning the magazine to study the picture more closely, 'and the article is pure Berlin fantasy. If half the things she says about Bruno Xavier are true———'

'Stop, Sophie, please!' Louise pushed her dark hair backwards, closing her eyes. She felt physically defiled, insulted by the article. Not for her own sake, but for Bruno's. 'He must have been nauseated,' she said in a low voice.

'Apparently he was furious,' Sophie nodded. 'But that edition of the magazine sold out, naturally.'

'God,' Louise groaned, 'this makes things a thousand times worse . . .'

'What things?' Sophie asked sharply.

'My article. Oh, damn . . .' She looked up hopelessly at Sophie's puzzled expression. 'I've just sent off an article about Bruno.' Tiredly, she explained the whole situation as concisely as she could.

'But I can't understand why you're so upset about it,' Sophie exclaimed when she'd finished. 'You're a journalist, Louise. A damn good one. What's more, he knew you were a journalist when he first met you. The man would be a fool to tell anything to a reporter and not expect her to use it—and I don't think Bruno Xavier's that much of a fool!'

'We had something special,' Louise said miserably, shaking her head. 'A kind of intimacy. I don't know how to explain it.' She looked blankly round the little bar. 'He wouldn't have expected me to make an article out of what he told me. It was a confidence.'

'I don't want to bring you down any further, Lou,' Sophie said, smiling slightly, 'but Bruno Xavier has special relationships with a lot of women. Like *Fraulein* Ackermann, for example.' Louise winced painfully. 'Look—I know you feel a lot for him, but that's the kind of man he is. *Un beau tigre.* Women adore him, all women. That's why that little bitch Ackermann wrote the article—to make a quick fortune. D'you think I wouldn't jump into his bed if he so much as nodded?' She studied the downcast, glossy head, her expression affectionate. 'Come on, Lou.' She tilted Louise's face upwards, and was dismayed to see that the green eyes were wet with tears. 'Lou! *Oh, mon Dieu*, honey—don't be like this!'

'Oh, Sophie, I hate myself,' she choked.

'For the love of God, *why*?' Mingled frustration and sympathy made Sophie's dark French face wrinkle up like an old woman's. 'You've just landed one of the biggest fish in the reporting world, and you're behaving as though the end of the world has come!'

'Sorry,' she said shakily, screwing a tissue into her eyes. The tears had been swelling behind her lids the whole day, since her departure from Catánia airport at ten a.m. with her heart aching. At last they had simply spilled out. They'd brought no relief, leaving her feeling more wretched than ever.

'There's nothing to be sorry about,' Sophie said, glaring at a curious Spanish reporter who'd been staring their way. 'Here—finish my Dubonnet.' Louise gulped the sweet stuff down obediently, feeling its welcoming burn in her stomach. 'Did he specifically tell you *not* to use the story?' Sophie demanded.

'No,' Louise admitted. 'But I didn't even ask for his permission, either!'

'Well, look at it this way,' Sophie went on reasonably. 'Bruno may be angry with you—but so what? By now you know that these things are part of any journalist's life. Whatever you write, someone's going to bitch about it, no? But you'll never see the guy again. So why the big guilt-complex?'

'Because Bruno means something special to me,' Louise said, staring dully at the evening outside. 'And I am going to see him again—tomorrow. I'm supposed to be spending the day on *Merope* with him.' Sophie's eyes widened. 'But I don't know how I can face him, Sophie. I'm no better in my way than Laura Ackermann! No other man has ever meant as much to me—and I had to go and do this to him . . .'

'I see.' She cupped her pointed chin in both hands, and watched Louise. 'I *see*. He made love to you yesterday, yes?' she asked gently. Louise shook her head in tired bewilderment.

'Of course not. I told you—we went diving at Naxos.'

'I rather thought,' Sophie said tentatively, 'from the evident intimacy of your conversation, that you might have made all that up as a convenient cover-story.'

'And that I'd wormed the story out of him in bed?'

Sophie nodded, then looked embarrassed at Louise's viridian glare, and pointed to the magazine. 'Well, *ma chérie*, these things do happen——'

'Not to me,' Louise snapped. 'It just turned out like that, I don't pretend to know why. He told me he *trusted* me.' The recollection of it made her lip tremble again, and she closed her eyes, shaking her head. 'God, I've been such a fool. When he finds out, he won't ever want to speak to me again!'

Understanding dawned at last in Sophie's face.

'Louise—you're in love with him!'

'That's impossible,' Louise smiled, her mouth wry. 'I've only met him three or four times.'

'With some men, that's more than enough,' Sophie said seriously. 'But you don't imagine he feels anything for you, do you?' Louise's silence answered the question, and Sophie sat back in consternation. 'But—I mean—*Bruno Xavier*—Louise, the man has literally dozens of women! Like I told you, he's a *beau tigre*, someone who hunts to kill. He's never showed the slightest trace of affection for one of them—why should he start with you? As soon as he gets bored with you, it'll be on to the next conquest——'

Louise listened in weary silence, knowing that Sophie was only trying to help. But she'd seen the way Bruno had looked at her, and she'd have staked her very life on the fact that he didn't regard her simply as a potential sexual conquest. Laura Ackermann's filth hadn't changed that by one iota. Maybe it was nothing more than a friendly interest—but to Louise Jordan, Bruno Xavier's interest was enough to change her whole life.

The trouble was that the whole thing could only be described as a miracle.

And people didn't believe in miracles anymore.

'Listen to me, *ma chérie*, I'm really worried about you!' Sophie shook Louise's hand earnestly. 'You're too sweet, too lovely to throw your happiness away on a Don Juan like Bruno. Leave him to the Laura Ackermanns. If it were me, I'd know how to handle myself—enjoy every second while it lasts, commit myself to absolutely nothing, have no regrets when it ends—and dream about it for the rest of my life. But you—you're a soft-core woman. Too easily hurt to play games like these.'

'It isn't a game,' she said gently.

'You see what I mean,' Sophie groaned. 'Why the hell did you wait so damned long to fall in love?' she cursed. 'And why the hell did you have to choose Bruno Xavier?'

'I didn't know there was any choice involved,' Louise said sadly.

'Of course there is. Look at me—I fell in love at sixteen.'

'With the professional golfer at the course near the school,' Louise nodded, trying to smile. 'I remember.'

'Well, I've had practise. You haven't. As for your going to the yacht tomorrow, I'd advise you to develop a sudden chill——' She broke off as David Lomax arrived, his world-weary face smiling, to tell them the latest piece of outrageous gossip that was doing the rounds of a tense and slightly bored news community.

Not really wanting to hear any more of Sophie's well-meant advice, Louise sat and talked as cheerfully as she could for half-an-hour, then excused herself, saying she had a headache, and was going back to her hotel to sleep. She needed to think, decide on what the best thing to do was.

Her heart sank at the sight of the fat telegram waiting under her door. It was, as she'd expected, from Percy Widows:

'Bruno Xavier story and photographs superb. Printing story entire this issue, your earlier portrait on cover,' it began. Louise bit her lip sharply. That photograph would be on every newsagent's stand, in every supermarket and bookshop throughout Britain. She sank on to the bed, reading on. *'This is your best work ever, repeat, best ever. Imperative you send follow-up article dealing with the years between as soon as possible. Am discussing syndication with U.S. network, possible television tie-in later on. This will be a lot bigger than the Ackermann episode, and a lot classier. I shall resist asking how exactly you came by story, but hope you enjoyed every minute of it.*

Dinner at Savoy when you get back. Repeat it is imperative you follow up with more Xavier material as soon as possible. Neglect Etna if necessary, consider Xavier your main target.

Good hunting, very best wishes, Percy.

She lay back on the bed, letting the telegram rustle to the floor. *Good hunting.* The irony of it was sharp as steel in her side. The peak of her career so far—and the lowest she had ever sunk in her own self-estimation.

The chambermaid had carefully gathered all her scattered notes for the article, and stacked them neatly on the little writing-desk. She stared at them dully, wishing she'd never even begun that story.

A follow-up article? Percy didn't know what he was asking for! She punched the pillow restlessly into shape, and lay still, thinking hard.

Had she been right when she'd accused herself of being no better than Laura Ackermann? How could she completely condemn herself for simply doing her job well? Journalism, by necessity, meant prying into other people's lives, sometimes against their will. Many successful journalists regularly employed tricks infinitely worse than her own mild subterfuge. The Ackerman article was a prime example. And her own story was so good. Maybe even, as Percy had said, the best thing she'd ever done; and journalism wasn't just a career with her—it was a vocation. No, her anguish didn't lie in that—it stemmed from the growing realisation that she had probably lost Bruno for ever.

Never once in two years had she found her career clashing with her own womanhood like this. Being a woman and being a photojournalist had seemed to mesh together so naturally; now, she felt as though she were being torn apart. Being a photojournalist had always meant being with the cream of her profession to Louise—a newswoman who not only wrote, but who took the pictures to go with her articles. It had been an ambition that had started in her very early teens, when her father had first kindled the love of photography in her. John Jordan had been a magician—literally. In between pulling rabbits out of hats at children's parties and pantomimes, he'd been a talented amateur photographer; and it had been in his makeshift darkroom under the stairs at the house in Erith that Louise had first been spellbound by that other magic—the scientific magic of chemicals and light called photography.

She hadn't known, of course, that her father was alreay dying when he'd bought her her first camera for her fourteenth birthday. By her fifteenth, though, he'd been dead for two months, and her life had changed for ever, leaving her suddenly serious, and far more aware of the future ahead of her than most fifteen-year-olds. What had remained, though, had been the knowledge and skill which John Jordan had ingrained in her, and her innate ability to write lucidly, grippingly, and fast.

Qualities which Percy Widows had instantly seen in the self-possessed young woman who'd come to him for a job, straight from a college diploma in journalism. Those on the *Women Today* staff who'd sneered that the normally dour Percy had finally been bewitched—by a pair of sparkling green eyes—had been permanently silenced by the work Louise had started turning in—work that was marked by a perception and an attention to quality far above Louise's years.

But she could never have anticipated that this very skill, the thing she did best, would ever stand in the way of her own happiness. But she was at last beginning to understand Percy Widows' often-repeated warning that journalism would one day force her to choose between success and friendship.

She curled up, exhaustion lying heavy on her lids. The single glaring fact in all the confusion, the fact that had been responsible for all her unhappiness over the past twelve hours, was that she could no longer carry on as though nothing had happened. She couldn't face Bruno, knowing that in London the lay-out editors

would already be designing the six-page spread for
maximum impact ... She would either have to tell him
what she'd done, or avoid him altogether. Otherwise the
revelation, when it inevitably came, would be all the
more terrible. A pang of pity for him made her wince
sharply. He was like a lion, majestic and free, yet
followed by a thousand jackals and lesser parasites
hoping to gather some scraps in his wake.

And she had just become one of them. She thought
sadly of the unbelievable depths in those grey eyes.

Semplicità ...

What a joke.

'If you're feeling ill,' Bruno said, his voice losing none
of its velvety urgency down the telephone, 'then I
definitely want to see you. I'll come to your hotel.'

'I don't—er——' She squeezed her eyes shut against
the morning sun, aching to see him, feel his presence.
Her dreams of the night before had been full of his face
and voice. Trying to put him off was one of the hardest
things she'd ever done.

'You've seen a doctor, yes?'

'Well, not actually——' Her clumsy lie about food
poisoning was becoming more and more transparent,
and he cut through her stammering with a touch of
Corsican steel.

'Louise, I don't understand.' The bewitching accent
was more pronounced, making him sound more
foreign. 'Are you trying to avoid seeing me? I would
rather you simply said so if you are.'

'No,' she denied, biting her lip. 'No, I'm dying to see
you, Bruno——'

'Then stop all this silliness,' he said, and the sound of
the smile in his voice was enough to make her go weak

at the knees. 'I've given the crew the day off. We'll be alone on *Merope*, just you and me. If you don't feel so well, we can just lie in the sun, or laze in the water—whatever you please. There are salads in the gallery, everything prepared. You don't have to do anything you don't want to. But you'll certainly feel a lot better out in the fresh air than you will cooped up in a hotel room.'

'Oh, Bruno——'

'And if you're worrying about *madre* Etna, I assure you that the view from my yacht will be even more spectacular than from Taormina.'

'Well——'

'Take a taxi down to Mazzaró,' he commanded. 'I'll wait for you in the launch, down at the fisherman's pier.' His voice deepened into a husky caress. 'I want to see you, little bee.'

'I want to see you,' she shivered, eyes closed.

'In half an hour, then.' The line clicked dead, and she put the receiver down miserably. So much for her noble resolution of last night. She wasn't going to be able to stay away from him, no more than a magnetic needle could avoid pointing north. He had already become an addiction with her.

She packed her cameras into the bulky bag, thinking how remote Etna seemed now, how inconsequential the question of an eruption had become, stuffed towels and bikini on top of them, and almost ran down to the square to find a taxi. On the winding, precipitous drive down, she stared out at the azure sea below, glittering in the morning sun. *Merope* lay in a dazzling sheet of sunlight, her exquisite white shape almost hidden in the glaze beyond Isolabella.

Nothing could stop her heart singing at the sight, and

at the thought of being with Bruno soon. Maybe today, she thought with a bittersweet tremor, maybe just for today I can pretend nothing's happened, and the world's still perfect.

And oh, he made her feel so good!

Ruthlessly, she thrust all guilty knowledge to the furthermost recesses of her mind. There would be time for guilt. Later.

Her heart surged as she saw the slim white launch already moored at the end of the little pier, like a white gull drifting on the cobalt water.

He was waiting for her in the launch, an excitingly male figure in denims and a raw linen shirt open to reveal the bronze of his chest.

'Hi,' she called as she reached the end of the pier, breathless as much from the sight of him as from the run.

'You look a picture!' He looked up at her with a half-smile from the boat, his eyes glinting. Without much thought, she'd pulled on tattered shorts cut off from a snug-fitting pair of old denims and a cool white T-shirt that clung to her perfect breasts rather more revealingly than she normally liked. She'd wondered whether it was all too casual and daring for a day with Bruno; but those amused, appreciative grey eyes told her uncompromisingly that her outfit was a success!

He took her bag, then lifted her down into the launch as lightly as though she were a feather.

'Your cameras weigh more than you do, little bee,' he said softly, staring into her eyes. He didn't release her, but drew her against the teak-hard strength of his body, oblivious of the interested sun-worshippers along the pier. She clung to his arms, spellbound, her lips parting tremulously as she saw the controlled desire in his slow smile. 'You don't look very sick,' he remarked in a velvety purr, taking in the clear, warm green depths of her eyes, the honey-coloured glow of her skin.

'Perhaps you've made me better,' she suggested in a voice that was almost a whisper.

He kissed her gently, his lips firm and sun-warm against her own, making her knees suddenly turn to water. Weakness made her lean against him, the taut power in his male body completing the devastation that his mouth had brought to her senses. Her lips began to part under his, the moistness of her inner mouth yielding to him, when a chorus of applause and whistles from the little crowd on the pier made him draw back. Now his smile was deep as the Mediterraenan itself, his eyes cloudy with some undefined passion.

'We'd better go before the *carabinièri* decide to arrest us for making a public nuisance,' she suggested. With elegant grace, he led her to the wheel. Weak as a kitten, Louise subsided into the leather seat beside him, realising that nothing and no one had ever affected her as this man did. He seemed to shake her very soul as easily as he could scatter a handful of water in the sun! The engines rumbled into life as he pressed the starter; he steered the launch carefully through the dancing waves around the pier, then speeded up as they made for the white yacht, lying tranquil half a mile out to sea.

'You'll have to make do with my own humble services today,' he informed her. 'I've given the crew three days off.' She looked at the hard profile quickly, and he raised one black eyebrow. 'Don't worry, *piccolina*—your virtue will be safe with me.' He glanced at her bare legs with a wicked glint. 'More or less.'

The colour mounted to her cheeks, and she reached

up to trap her dark hair, blown into a tangle by their speed, and pulled it into a quick ponytail.

'When you do that,' he grinned, 'you look about seventeen. How old are you exactly?'

'Twenty-two,' she said after a moment's hesitation.

'Twenty-two.' His mouth turned down in mock-bitterness. 'I'm fourteen years older than you, Louise Jordan. Does that put you off?'

'Of course not,' she said innocently. 'I've always liked older men.'

The eyebrow lifted again. 'Indeed?'

'Not that you're old,' she blurted in sudden horror, dismayed by what she'd said. 'You're just right—I mean——'

'*Semplicitá,*' he said with a soft laugh, reaching for her hand. Her skin shivered as his fingers interlaced with hers. 'You couldn't offend me if you tried.'

The Italian word brought back her hidden guilt with an abrupt jolt, and she looked away, to the approaching yacht, her hand clasped in his. Her heart was suddenly heavy despite the brilliant sun.

True to his word, *Merope* was peaceful and deserted. The little dinghy tied by a painter to her stern scarcely bobbed on the calm sea, and Bruno tied the launch alongside the dinghy, slinging a rubber tyre over the immaculate side of the launch to prevent the boats bumping. *Merope*'s gleaming brasswork and snowy paint testifying to the loving care of her crew.

'She's so beautiful,' Louise marvelled, looking around the quarterdeck. 'She's a dream.'

'Yes,' he nodded, leading her under the canvas awning which cast a cool shade over one end of the deck, '*Merope*'s my second home. You'd better leave your precious cameras here, in case Etna decides to erupt this morning.'

She obeyed, putting the equipment on a wrought-iron table. 'Where is your real home, then?' she asked. *'Le Faucon?'*

'Ultimately, yes.' His eyes were thoughtful. 'But *Le Faucon* is abandoned. It is only home to the winds now. I *live* in Rome, just off the Via Condotti.' Lithe and graceful, he ushered her into the fabulous stateroom. 'A drink?'

'Just orange, please.' She kicked off her sandals and wandered across the luxuriously thick carpet, studying the magnificent furniture and paintings. 'The Via Condotti,' she murmured, searching her memory, and coming up with an image of a glittering street in the heart of Rome's most beautiful and fashionable area. 'That's a very impressive address, isn't it?'

'If big cities impress you,' he agreed.

'Rome isn't just a big city!' She accepted the dewy glass. 'It's the capital of Europe. How I envy you, living there . . .'

He touched her satiny mouth with a smile, than toasted her silently. 'I prefer *Merope*, I assure you. I own an apartment in an eighteenth century *palazzo*, overlooking the Spanish Steps.' He drank from his glass, then shrugged. 'It is beautiful, elegant. Soulless.'

'Then why don't you give it soul?' she demanded.

'For that, little bee, one needs a woman's touch.'

'Surely that isn't a problem, *signor?*' she suggested with a touch of irony in the lowering of her thick lashes. 'Judging by what they say, you have enough women in your life to furnish a hundred eighteenth century apartments.'

'Alas,' he countered with a wicked gleam, 'their average stay is too fleeting to have much more impact than the rearranging of bedclothes.'

For some reason the comment lashed on tender nerves. 'Then you *are* a roué,' she snapped, her cheeks flaming.

He met her angry green eyes with cool grey indifference. 'If that is what you would have me. I'm merely living up to the image you seem to expect of me.'

'It's true, though, isn't it?' she said, her whole being aching for his denial.

'It was you, and not I, who opened this line of banter,' he reminded her without answering her question. 'If you are angry, you have no one to blame but yourself.' She turned away from him, irrationally upset, and looked around the stateroom, her glass cradled in her hands.

'You are right, of course.' She gestured at the gilt furnishings, changing the subject with an effort. 'Your apartment—is it like this?'

'No. It's ultra-modern, Roman style. All blacks and whites and greys. Tubular steel and white hide. High-technology fittings. There's even a computer terminal in the bedroom.'

'It doesn't sound very warm,' she agreed. 'Yet in a way that suits you as well as this classical opulence. You're a man of the present, *Signor* Xavier. A man of the new age.'

His laugh was husky, intimate. 'So many questions, and only twenty-two.' He took her arm, making her feel terribly juvenile and ingenuous and led her to the doorway leading to the cabins. 'And for God's sake, call me Bruno. You can have one of the guest cabins for today,' he went on, leading her to one of the panelled doors in the corridor. 'Why not change into your costume now? If you're feeling well enough, we can lie in the sun until midday.'

She obeyed, and closed the cabin door behind her. It was luxurious, on a scale with the great stateroom. The shot silk furnishings made it very obviously a woman's cabin, designed with a woman's delicate tastes in mind. She surveyed herself in the full-length salmon-tinted mirror, and pulled a jealous face. A very vain woman, no doubt as beautiful as the dawn, and as moral as an alley cat.

Some thoughtful hand had laid out everything for her—soap, towels, suntan lotion, even a meltingly soft towelling-robe in purest white. She stroked the robe, loving him for his kindness, and almost forgiving him for the dawn-beautiful alley-cat of her imagination.

Louise pulled off her clothes, noting that she'd lost a little weight over the past few days. Since meeting Bruno, she'd resisted the delicious and ubiquitous *pasta* dishes of Sicily in favour of salads and seafood, and the difference to her golden thighs and tummy was perceptible. She had brought her only other swimming-costume today, a one-piece in metallic turquoise that made up for its overall modesty by plunging dramatically at the back and clinging to her youthful figure like a second skin.

With a last nervous glance in the mirror, she picked up a huge, fluffy beach-towel that had been laid on the bed, and went out on to the quarterdeck to find Bruno.

He was already lying on his stomach in the sun, wearing only the same narrow black costume as he'd worn at Naxos. The sight of his near-naked body, golden and powerful in the sun, made her stop short, her mouth dry. He raised himself on one elbow, looking at her from under sun-narrowed coal-black lashes.

'You found everything?'

'Yes,' she gulped, walking uncertainly over to him.

The mahogany deck was hot under her bare feet, the sunlight a benediction on her satiny skin. 'You're a very kind man.'

He rolled on to his back, leaning on his elbows. '*Man tut was man kann,*' he grinned, his smile a sabre-flash of white against his tan. The German reminded her sharply of Laura Ackermann, and suddenly the sight of his magnificent body at her feet sent a shudder through her that made her settle hastily on to her bottom on the warm deck beside him, tearing her gaze away from him. Damn the horrible woman! How *dare* she accept love from this staggeringly beautiful body, and defile it all for the sake of mere money?

She gasped in surprise as his fingers tugged the straps of her costume off her shoulders.

'You've shivering like a frightened dog,' he commented gently. 'I'm just going to put some oil on your shoulders—not even your delicious tan is going to stop that exquisite skin from burning in this sun.' She hung her head forward, holding the costume from sliding off her breasts as his strong, sure fingers massaged the oil across her shoulders, moulding the delicate muscles in her neck and back. Did he know what he did to her, she wondered weakly, her heart twisting inside her at the sheer sensuality of his touch.

'You smell sweet,' he said softly, lying down beside her and closing his eyes, leaving her skin like burnished gold in the sun. 'What is it?'

'Opium,' she answered, studying him covertly through almost-closed lashes. His body was mature, the muscles under the velvety skin hard-looking, supremely fit. She yearned to reach out and caress the crisp black hair that ran from his broad chest down the plane of his flat, taut stomach. It would be like caressing a panther's coat. And would, she thought with a pang, probably have the same result—instant destruction for Louise Jordan!

'Lie down,' he commanded huskily, eyes flickering open to reveal smoky amethysts that reached into her soul. 'I don't want those green cat's eyes on me.'

'Why not?' she asked in embarrassment at having been surprised staring at him.

'Because,' he said, a sudden blaze in his eyes, 'you're too beautiful for comfort.'

She obeyed, not understanding. It was blissfully peaceful in the sun, only the lapping of the sea disturbing the silence.

'You're so lucky,' she said dreamily, pillowing her cheek on her hands. 'I've always dreamed about having a yacht.'

'I never have enough time with my *Merope*,' he smiled. 'The days are too short, even in midsummer. I have to go back in a few days.'

It was as though thunder had suddenly struck out of the cloudless sky.

'Back?' she whispered. 'Where to?'

'Rome.'

She lay in stunned silence. It hadn't occurred to her that he would ever be leaving; the exquisite white yacht had seemed like a castle to her, immovable and fixed. Suddenly aware of the regular movement beneath her that proclaimed *Merope* a living, wandering creature of the sea, she tried to fight back the tears that pressed against her tightly-shut lids.

'Why did you come?' she asked, keeping her voice as even as she could. 'To see the volcano?'

'Partly,' he replied carelessly. 'I stopped on my way to Cyprus, though I had no real destination in mind—

none except freedom, and the sea.' He glanced at her. 'But my free time is drawing to an end.'

She digested this in silence. 'How does a man with so many commitments find the time for even a few days?' she asked, striving for flippancy.

'I needed a break badly,' he said quietly. 'My life wearied me.'

'What,' she asked, opening her eyes to look at his profile, so close to her own, 'with all that wealth?'

'You think wealth is important to human happiness?'

'Well——' she blinked, taken aback by the directness of his question, 'no, I don't.'

'Nor do I,' he shrugged.

She sat up, crossing her legs, staring down at the passionate curve of his mouth. 'What makes you work, then,' she demanded, 'if not money?'

He smiled slowly, rising on one elbow with introspective eyes. 'Why? For one thing, I like to make an impact on the world around me.'

'In what way?'

'I love to see the chaos of a construction site slowly turn into a brand new building, a place for people to work and live and do things. I like to see books being printed, trees being planted, machines being made. I like to have people with purpose around me, planning, designing, doing. I like to see men working, not standing in dole queues.' He paused, studying his broad, capable hands, then went on, almost to himself, 'I like to see a rundown community find new hope, pick themselves up and begin to flourish. I like to see things happen, and know that I made them happen!' He met Louise's eyes. 'I love to see things grow, new, healthy, vigorous things. That gives me pleasure, little bee. Not money.'

Ashamed at her own crass question, Louise looked down shyly. 'I see.' She bit her lip, knowng know that she'd misjudged him badly on an earlier question. 'I don't suppose you really get much kick out of casual sex, either?'

'Nor that, either,' he agreed in a soft voice. 'Despite what the gossip columnists write.' He smiled tiredly. 'Why they've chosen to lavish all their frustrated sexual fantasies on me I'll never know.'

She laid her cheek against his arm, not daring to look up at him. 'Can I ask one more question?'

'If you must,' he smiled.

'Then tell me—what exactly in your life wearied you?' His fingers closed with unexpected ruthlessness in her hair, tugging it reprovingly.

'What is this,' he grinned, 'an interview, little bee?'

'No.'

'Good.' He rose, fluid as a jaguar, and hauled her to her feet. 'Enough about me, then. Come—let's swim!'

CHAPTER FIVE

IT was a blissful afternoon. The water was cool and made translucent as glass by the brilliant sunshine, and Louise revelled in it like a child, splashing in the sheltered lee of *Merope*, diving beside him into the glassy depths, where the bottom seemed littered with pearls. Later in the afternoon, she lay, languourous and wet, on an air-mattress, and floated dreamily on the undulating waves, talking to him with an intimacy she'd never known before, not even with Sophie Dubarry. Talking about Louise Jordan . . .

He wanted to know everything—about her sunny childhood in Erith, her mother and father, her schooldays. How she'd learned the technical business of photography on summer week-ends, and in the tiny darkroom under the stairs. About her father's illness, the terrible impact of his death, the deep changes that had been wrought in her life by his absence. About her new sense of purpose, her need to have a goal in life. About college, the boys she'd known there——

'I wasn't all that popular,' she assured him.

'I find that very hard to believe,' he smiled, floating bronzed and reassuring beside her, 'unless English men are even colder and duller than they're reputed to be?'

She gurgled with laughter. 'You're very unkind, Bruno. I was one of those hard-working girls who're always too busy to go anywhere,' she confessed. 'I was never out of the darkrooms or books full of technical data. It wasn't until I joined *Women Today* that I really

101

began to get some fun out of life. Not *that* kind of fun,'
she retorted, amused by his wickedly raised eyebrow, 'I
mean—oh, seeing the world, meeting lots of people,
getting around . . .'

She told him about Percy Widows; craggy and
uncompromising, the man who'd been something like a
father-figure to her for the past two years—a man
difficult to really like, but easy to respect. The subject
of her own article about Bruno was drifting ominously
close as she told him the sort of work she did, and she
found herself with all the lazy relaxation leaving her
body, on the brink of wanting to tell him everything.

'You——' She hesitated, trailing her fingers in the
cool sea, watching him with half-closed eyes. 'I suppose
you don't have much of an opinion of journalists?'

'They're an occupational hazard,' he replied, amused
by her question. He laid a cool, wet hand on her golden
back. 'You're going to roast, *cara*—let's get you into
the shade, and have some lunch.'

Under the awning, Bruno dried her back with a
practised skill that reminded her angrily of the alley-cat
for a few seconds—before sensual pleasure took over.
He helped her wrap herself in the white robe; it set her
green eyes and tanned skin off with a very feminine
perfection, and his eyes were bright as he watched her
comb her water-darkened hair into glistening order.

'Some journalists are easier on the eye than others,'
he said softly, taking her shoulders and touching her
nose with his lips, leaving her with a suddenly pounding
heart. 'Come and have some salad. What made you ask
that question, by the way? Insecurity?'

'In a way,' she replied, following him into the
stateroom. She curled up on a green velvet *chaise-longue*
watching him, and again hesitated, afraid to ask the

question that was uppermost in her mind. 'Someone showed me an article yesterday,' she began tentatively. 'In a German magazine called *Berlin*. By someone called Laura Ackermann.'

'Ah, *die anständige Fräulein* Laura.' His expression barely changed—she'd been expecting an eruption—but she sensed, rather than saw, the tensing of strong muscles across his shoulders. He belted the dark blue robe around his waist, not looking at her. 'I trust you enjoyed the story?'

'It was horrible,' she blurted out, unable to keep the emotion out of her voice. He glanced at her, grey eyes piercing, then smiled slightly.

'How beautiful you look in all this Baroque opulence, little bee. You might have been born a princess.'

She nodded, not wanting to leave the subject. 'Weren't you hurt by what that awful woman did to you?'

'It wasn't exactly pleasant,' he said drily. He turned and stared with hard eyes across the sunlit water outside. 'But if I was hurt, then I deserved it.'

'Why?'

'I was careless,' he said shortly. 'Careless and stupid. I should have recognised Laura for what she was.'

'She's very beautiful,' Louise said in a small voice, suddenly thinking with pain of Bruno in bed with someone else.

'She moves with a beautiful crowd,' he said harshly. He met her eyes. 'Despite what people say, Louise, I don't hop from bed to bed. Laura Ackermann fooled me completely. She's very good at what she does—she made me feel sorry for her, told me a heartbreaking story about being addicted to hard drugs, needing someone to help her out of the abyss.' He thrust his hands into the pockets of his gown, and leaned back against the desk. 'I swallowed the whole thing,' he said, his eyes full of self-anger. 'Taking pity on her seemed so natural. She knew exactly how to worm her way into my confidence, though I barely knew her. There was no shortage of so-called friends, either, to encourage the relationship.' He laughed softly, shaking his head. 'You must think me a complete fool?'

'No,' she said quietly. 'Nobody can be on the defensive all their lives.'

'So,' he shrugged, 'the next thing I knew, she was in my bed. The whole affair must have been planned like a military operation.' The bronzed face was cold, the leashed anger in his eyes an almost tangible force. 'We spent a few days together, went out to a few places—then she suddenly disappeared to Berlin, with some transparent story about a sick relation. Only then did I begin to realise how stupid I'd been. I couldn't work out exactly what Laura's idea was—and then the *Berlin* article came out.' He grimaced, acrid lines etched round his mouth. 'It was like having a can of rotten garbage dumped over me.'

'I'm so sorry,' she said miserably. 'What did you do?'

'I was angry,' he said quietly, and she knew instinctively that that was a severe understatement. 'For a few days, I wanted only to hit back. I have the economic muscle to crush *Berlin* completely, force it out of the publishing world——' Again, he shrugged bitterly, his accent becoming more harsh. 'What would that have achieved? One should be above such things. Besides, I hear that friend Laura has retired on her earnings, and is living like a queen in the Bahamas. So I came on holiday, instead.' The anger faded from his eyes as he looked at her, and there was a thrilling tenderness in his smile. 'Which was probably the best decision I ever made in my life, little bee.'

The implication in his words, which would have intoxicated her like hot wine in any other circumstances, merely added to her inner anguish now. 'After all that,' she whispered, close to tears, 'you still confided in me?'

He came over to her, and sat down beside her, warm passion in the amethyst eyes. 'You're as much like Laura as a hummingbird is like a cobra, Louise.' He caressed her cheek with infinite gentleness. 'I trust you, *amore mio* .'

'Oh, Bruno!' She melted into his embrace, squeezing her lids closed over the despair in her eyes. When he found out, when he found out ...

'What is it, baby?' he murmured, his lips close to her ear. 'Something's been troubling you all afternoon. Tell me what it is.' He lifted her face, and looked down into her swimming eyes. '*Dio*, I hate to see you cry! Is it me?'

'No,' she choked.

'Don't you trust me, little bee?' He kissed her wet lashes, the salt of her tears bringing a compassionate smile to the curve of his mouth. 'Ah, Louise—life's too short for tears.' He drew her close against him, the power of his arms infinitely comforting around her. 'I've never felt this with any woman, Louise,' he said quietly, his voice a rumble that seemed to pierce her whole body. 'To me, it's a kind of miracle. And the miracle is that I see the same thing happening in you, glowing in your eyes, trembling on your sweet lips.'

'Don't,' she begged, her heart feeling as though giant hands were tearing it apart inside her. Dear God, how could she ever tell him what she had done to him? 'Don't ...'

His mouth silenced hers with an authority which

obliterated all else. She clung to him, helpless, her lips parting under his, her yearning rising to meet him as she surrendered the sweetness of her inner mouth to his tongue. She'd never dreamed of a kiss like this, a possession that transcended every defence she had, parting all veils and disguises, so that it seemed to her dizzy soul that his mouth was caressing something deep inside her. As though their innermost beings were touching, fusing in a blaze of sunfire.

Shakily, she leaned back in his arms, her lips feeling bruised. His eyes were like Sicilian sun, almost too bright to look into. She slid her hand under the soft robe, her fingers spreading across the velvety skin of his chest, aware of the hard muscles beneath, feeling the pounding of his heart.

'Your mouth is honey-sweet,' he breathed, drawing her face to his again. 'I knew it would be ...' The urgency now in his kiss made her gasp out loud against his mouth, her hands reaching beneath his robe to cling to the naked power of his shoulders. His mouth was restless, fiercely desiring, never giving her the satisfaction she ached for. He claimed her lips teasingly, his tongue probing hers, his teeth sharp against her full lower lip; then he was kissing her eyes, her temples, the sensitive skin next to her ears, making her shudder uncontrollably, her lips forming his name again and again.

He drew the white robe away from her body, letting it fall in snowy folds against the *chaise-longue*. His touch was like an act of love in itself, hungry yet almost reverent, his eyes holding hers with tender command.

'*Ti voglio tanto bene,*' he said, his deep purr husky with desire.

'Oh, my love ...' No other language but Italian

would have a phrase like that, expressing the ache, the sweet undeniable longing that was almost love—that would soon be love. He eased the turquoise sheen of her costume away from her gilded shoulders, and she hung her head in shy passion as his rough intake of breath registered the way her naked breasts had affected him. His mouth was warm against her cool skin as he bent to her, tasting the sea-salt on the creamy swell of her breasts, making her cry out in a low moan as his lips brushed the aching peaks. His hair was still damp under her fingers, and she bowed over him, whispering his name shakily as his tongue firmed her nipples into almost unbearable tautness, leaving her soul aching and full, ready for love.

He shook his robe off impatiently, then drew her against the warmth of his naked skin, cradling her in his arms as though he knew instinctively how she was aching, how weak she felt. The moment was unbearably intimate, a sweet eternity crammed into minutes, their skin so close, so right, her honey against his bronze . . . He let her lie against him, his fingers caressing her cheek almost as though she were a child who needed comforting.

'Louise.' He said her name as though it were a prayer on his lips. 'Do you think this is all possible? That in a few short days, we could come to this?'

'It's a miracle,' she whispered, her lips against the crisp, dark hair of his chest. It was so intensely sweet to lie almost naked against him, her breasts pressed against his lithe virility, her fingers exploring, unforbidden, the dizzying new universe of his man's body. 'What else can it be?'

She raised wondering, deep green eyes to his, her parted lips timidly begging his kiss. With a soft laugh, he pulled her close, his body suddenly urgent as the spring of a hunting leopard against her. His kiss was ruthless, an almost overwhelming hunger mingling with his giving now. As though some potent drug had been poured into her veins, she pressed against him, her body offering itself to him in pagan need. The thrust of his desire was intoxicating, irresistibly exciting against her, making her want to surrender utterly to him, become his in body and soul.

She arched her neck as he kissed the tender hollow of her throat, turmoil filling her mind. She mustn't let this go on! This would only make things infinitely worse when the storm eventually broke. He'd think she'd offered him her body simply as Laura Ackermann had done before her—so that she would turn his lovemaking into a crude story, money in the bank.

'Oh, dear Heaven,' she whispered, 'stop now, before it's too late . . .' She clenched her fingers in his thick, dark hair, her body shaking with tortured passion. 'Bruno, don't do this to me!'

'Are you afraid?' he asked, smiling gently at her frantic expression.

'Afraid of you?' She caressed his face with trembling fingers, and shook her tousled head. 'Never, never my love——'

'Then why ask me to stop?' Supremely male, the desire burning in his eyes like flame, he crushed the reply on her lips, imprisoning her in the spell of his passion.

'No,' she pleaded, her body already responding helplessly, 'no, no . . .' He was unhurried, his touch confident and gentle despite the desire she could feel, taut as a hunter's bow against her. The stroke of his fingers was a preparation for love, guiding her inexperienced responses into the rip-tide of physical passion. A strong tide, strong as life, compelling as death. She had to resist this irresistible force, had to for her sake and his. The tension inside her curved to bursting-point, and she couldn't stop the scalding tears that spilled down her cheeks.

'Louise!' He stared in shock at her wet face, then drew her close, rocking her gently in his arms. 'What is it, child, for heaven's sake? Is it another man?'

'Nothing like that,' she answered, her voice uneven with tears. 'Oh, Bruno, I'm sorry.'

'Don't be sorry. Just tell me what it is.'

'I can't.' She clung to him, helpless to stop the tears. If only she had the courage to tell him now, get it over with, face his anger, try and find his forgiveness——

'I think it's time you got some rest,' he said softly, kissing her forehead. 'You've been under a strain, little bee. Too much sea, too much sun. And maybe too much love.'

'I'll be all right,' she begged, shaking the hair out of her eyes.

'No. You need sleep.' He kissed her lips once more, hard, then pulled the soft white beach-robe over her naked shoulders. His expression was wry, tender. 'Go to your cabin and dress. I'll take you home.'

He helped her to her feet, and watched her with thoughtful eyes as she walked, aching, back to her cabin to dress.

Sunday evening in the square. And the end of the most wonderful seven days of her life. The past week she'd spent with Bruno had been a sun-drenched heaven, starting with that day on the yacht, and extending through a succession of days filled with sea, sun—and Bruno.

And this day, the most perfect of all, had also been the most bittersweet for her. A day when the brilliance of love and life had been clouded by the thought of what the morrow was going to bring. A day on which the dream she'd let herself almost drown in was now coming to an end. She'd left Bruno only minutes ago, the print of his lips still warm on her own, to meet Sophie.

The hour of the *passaggio*, the evening stroll. The sidewalk cafés busy, the piazza full of peope walking, talking, meeting friends—it was all so perfect, so redolent of Italian life at its most gracious. Louise merely shrugged tautly when Sophie pointed that out, her slender fingers gripping the edge of the balustrade overlooking the sea, far down below in the dusk. A handful of distant pearls in the soft evening indicated where *Merope* lay at anchor, still as a painted ship on the ebb-tide.

'Lou,' Sophie said, laying a hand quietly on her friend's arm, 'I realise that this is none of my business, and that these past days have probably been heaven for you—I've hardly seen you—but I'm getting the feeling that this whole thing is getting out of control for you. I hate to feel you this tense and depressed.'

'It won't last long,' Louise said tersely, hating the muggy heat of the evening. '*Women Today* comes out tomorrow.' She tore her gaze away from the yacht's lights, and touched the beading of perspiration on her upper lip. Late afternoon had brought heavy masses of cloud from the south, and a stormy, pregnant atmosphere was settling in, promising a violent thunderstorm soon. Despite the cool dress she wore, with barely anything beneath it, she felt hot, nervously irritable.

Sophie lit a cigarette, and exhaled a plume of smoke into the heavy air.

'You spent the whole day with him again?' she asked.

Louise nodded dully. 'He took me to Piazza Armerina.' It had been a beautiful day. After seeing the magnificent Roman villa with its glittering mosaic floors, they'd wandered through the olive-groves, arm in arm, like lovers. She'd been able to keep her secret shadow well to the back of her mind, simply adoring him, delighting in the kaleidoscopic pleasure of his company. He'd made her laugh till she ached, then changed the laughter into gasping desire with a touch of a kiss, or even a shift in the dark light of his smile. More than ever before, she'd been aware of falling in love with him.

'It's a strange feeling,' she said quietly, turning her back on the sea, and staring with unseeing eyes at the bright lights that had been hung in the trees of the piazza. 'It really *is* like falling, Sophie. Like throwing yourself out of an airplane—an endless, wonderful free-fall that takes you deeper and deeper . . .'

'*C'est ça.*' There was almost envy in Sophie's dark eyes as she smiled at Louise. 'You've found the real thing, my dear. So what now?'

'I don't know.' There was a glimmer of lightning to the south, maybe a hint of the coming storm. Louise shook her head. 'I just don't know.' Her mind shied away from tomorrow by drifting back to yesterday, the hottest day of all. They'd driven through the sunlit countryside, she resting her head against his shoulder, dreaming that this could never end. Mile after mile of fragrant, bird-loud summer, redolent of wild thyme and briar-roses. They'd lain in a field of golden-ripe wheat, bright with scarlet poppies, and sky-blue cornflowers; they'd found wild cyclamens, hiding moistly sensual pink petals in the shade; jasmine, sweet basil, and forget-me-nots. They hadn't needed many words—smiles and kisses, and the lingering caresses of ready desire had been enough ... She shook the delicious memories away. Time to say goodbye to all that. 'Wait and see,' she said aloud. 'What else can I do?'

'Don't you think you might be getting the whole thing slightly out of proportion?' Sophie protested. 'Why should he be so angry with you, after all?'

'Maybe he wouldn't have been in normal circumstances. But what Laura Ackermann did to him really hurt. It's a raw place, Sophie. You should have seen his eyes when he was telling me about it.' She shuddered, remembering that cold grey fire. 'Soon he'll feel that way about me, too.'

'Then phone him up! Ring him on the ship-to-shore right now, and tell him!'

'What for?' She shrugged hopelessly. 'It's much too late. I decided a week ago to enjoy what was left of it, Sophie. Not spoil what I had with him. Now that time has run out, and I have to face the music.'

'Maybe you've overestimated the way he'll react—badly,' Sophie said. 'Perhaps he'll understand what made you write that article. Maybe you're doing him wrong to be so afraid.'

'Maybe,' Louise acknowledged tightly. 'It's such a horrible mess.' She turned to Sophie with a twisted smile. 'You were right, Sophie. I know too little about men. I'm too inexperienced, too clumsy to know how to handle myself with Bruno. Maybe someone with a bit more *savoir faire* would have been able to pass it off, I don't know——'

'Maybe you're too honest.' Impulsively, Sophie kissed her cheek. 'And too young!'

'I've grown a hundred years in the past fortnight.' She leaned back against the railing, picking up her heavy hair with both hands to cool her graceful neck. The memories wouldn't stay out of her mind.

'Hell,' she whispered, close to tears. She turned her blurred eyes towards the red glow of Etna. 'When is that *damn* mountain going to erupt?' she demanded in a trembling voice.

'Hey, hey.' Sophie's arm was comforting around her tensed shoulders. 'Take it easy, Lou.'

'I hate waiting for things,' Louise said, her thick lashes wet with unshed tears. 'I hate this explosive atmosphere. I wish to Heaven it was over and done with!'

And she wasn't sure whether she meant Etna, the coming storm, or Bruno Xavier.

The storm broke at ten o'clock that night, just as Louise was coming home early from an unhappy evening at a restaurant with David and Sophie. The distant rumblings of thunder had deepened like approaching artillery, and she just reached the jasmine-covered portico of the hotel in time before the first heavy, warm drops began to fall.

The rain was lashing against her windows by the time she'd undressed, and was lying back on her bed, naked except for nylon briefs. Her thoughts flew irresistibly to Bruno on board *Merope*. She could almost hear the rain pattering on the deck, feel the heavier swell of the sea beneath the deep keel. Cool air blew raindrops through her open shutters, bringing some relief to her hot skin, and she closed her eyes.

She awoke much later to the sound of the shutters

banging in the breeze. The storm was past, rumbling out to sea now, heading for mainland Italy. She got up stiffly, and closed the shutters. She was cold enough to get under the sheets now, the material almost rough against her nakedness. Memories of Bruno came with a shockingly powerful rush. God, she needed him, wanted him here now. Wanted the comfort of his arms, the dizzying power of his man's body.

Why hadn't she told him? The realisation of her stupidity came to her whole, in one piece, as though the release of the storm had cleared her eyes for the first time. She should have told him, the day after she'd sent that article to Percy Widows. She should have told him then, and risked his anger. By hiding it, by leaving him to find out for himself, she'd put everything at risk, a terrible risk she couldn't afford.

Sophie had been right. Rigid with anger and despair at her own folly, she squeezed her fists into her eyes. Why had realisation come so late? Had she really been so blinded by her growing love for Bruno that she hadn't done the only thing that might have kept him close to her?

She slumped back against the pillows, hopelessness overshadowing her thoughts. What was the use of worrying now? The copies of *Women Today*, glossy and new-smelling, were already being distributed. They'd be in every outlet across Britain. In all the foreign-language bookstalls throughout Italy and Sicily.

And sooner or later, someone would pass a copy on to Bruno.

Her sleep was fitful, chased by nightmares, and she woke up late, with a bad case of the blues. She glanced at her alarm clock. Eight forty-five. Bruno was going to be away today and tomorrow, and she was going to have to keep herself busy somehow. Perhaps it would be best to get out of Taormina today, away from everything.

Sitting cross-legged in bed, she picked up the bedside telephone, and asked the receptionist to put her through to the volcano research station at Adrano, only a few miles from Etna. She spoke to one of the deputy directors, a man with a youngish, pleasant voice who introduced himself as Dottore Pirandello, and who agreed readily to give her an interview later that morning. She put the receiver back feeling marginally better. At least she'd be working, and occupying her mind with something, even though the interview might not be newsworthy. She knew from long experience how reluctant experts were to commit themselves to anything at all.

Particularly, she thought in frustration, gazing at the cool, unmoved peak of Etna in the distance, when it came to something as unpredictable as a volcano.

The telephone rang back while she was dressing, and she picked it up with a sense of foreboding. It was Sophie, her voice full of delight.

'Lou? I've just got a copy of *Women Today*——'

'Where from?' Louise asked in dismay.

'Aldo's—the newsagent in the piazza—he gets all the foreign journals. Listen—your article's fantastic! It's a masterpiece, Louise—the best thing I've read this year.'

'Thanks,' Louise said dully. All she could think of was that her time was now running terribly short. Bruno would see that article today, tomorrow at the latest——

'Are you listening?'

'I'm listening,' she said, trying to inject some life into her response. 'I'm glad you like it, Sophie.'

'It nearly made me cry! Oh, Lou—it's so sensitive, so perceptive. I'm sure he'll love it. How could he possibly be offended?'

'I hope you're right,' Louise said with a heavy sigh, knowing that it wasn't the content that would offend him, but the article itself—the underhand way she'd gathered the material, the way she'd used a private conversation.

'Meet me for breakfast at *Casa Passarello*, okay?'

'I can't. I'm going up to the research station to interview someone there.'

'What for?' Sophie scorned. 'They won't tell you anything new. You're just running away!'

'Yes. Besides, it's work, isn't it? Anyway, I'll get some closer shots of Etna. Who knows,' she added with grim humour, 'the whole damn thing might go up while I'm there, and end all my troubles.'

'Trés amusant.'

'How about dinner at my hotel—around eight?'

'Okay. I'm dying to tell you all about your article— you little genius!'

She put the receiver down, smiling wryly, and finished dressing. In defiance of her nervous, depressed mood, she put on her most summery dress, a deep green frock patterned with thousands of tiny flowers, which left her shoulders and slender neck bare, and rustled coolly around her long legs.

On her breakfast tray, among the cold coffee and cereal, was a folded magazine, its wrapper postmarked London. She didn't open it, knowing what it was, just stuffed it into her bag for later reference, and ran down the stairs into the morning sun.

On her way down to Avis to rent a car for the day, Louise stopped to stare across the calm bay to where

Merope lay, fresh as paint against the cobalt sea. The storm had rinsed the world clean, leaving a joyful feeling in the air. A feeling Louise didn't share. She dragged her eyes away from the yacht, and hurried on.

At Avis she rented a brand-new Alfa, and set off towards Adrano, gloomily enjoying the feel of the sporty car, and keeping her thoughts resolutely off Bruno. Adrano was on the slopes of Etna itself, a small town which had been destroyed countless times by eruptions in the past. Despite her grim little joke to Sophie, Louise knew she'd be in no immediate danger. Unlike Krakatoa or Mount St Helens, Etna was not prone to the nuclear-equivalent explosions which could level hundreds of square miles in a split second. When the eruption came, the lava would flow at a steady five or ten miles an hour, slow enough to give ample time for evacuation.

Still, she couldn't help a recurrent squiggle of fear in her stomach as she drove towards the symmetrical white cone, the highest point on the whole island. No amount of logic could stop that primitive awe at the back of her mind, a feeling that must surely be left over from days when humans lived in caves, and when the whole Mediterranean was a violent volcanic area.

The land was abundantly fertile as she drove closer and higher; fresh lava could take up to fifty years to crumble into usable soil—but when it did so, the rich mineral content ensured that vines and olives and wheat grew strong and vigorous—one reason why the villagers always returned, even when the unpredictable rages of their mountain had destroyed virtually every possession they had. Lava, Louise knew, had flowed as far as Palermo and Catania in the past, a river of molten rock hot enough to make trees burst into flames a mile ahead of the flow. She'd seen the immense black slabs of cold lava lying vast in the fields outside the cities. Whole civilisations had been obliterated overnight elsewhere in the region—Pompeii, the Minoans, perhaps even that legendary place called by the ancients 'Atlantis'.

Adrano was even closer to Etna than she'd anticipated. The mountain towered over the town, a bare few kilometres away, and the height made it cold enough for Louise to regret her pretty frock. The streets seemed deserted, many of the shops boarded up, many of the shutters drawn. Most of the villagers had probably been evacuated long ago. The Volcano Research Station itself was a prefabricated structure just outside the town—designed, she guessed, to be dismantled at an hour's notice, and all the precious equipment carried to safety.

She locked the car in the car park, glancing uneasily up at the cone. Under her very feet, maybe waiting to explode right now, was a million tons of molten rock. She could see now that the cone itself was black volcanic sand, iced with perpetual snow. She shivered. Summer ended right here, no matter how baking the temperatures down at the coast. The plume of steam that hung over the mouth of Etna didn't reassure her in the slightest, and her instinctive feeling of panic persisted right through her reception by Dottore Pirandello in a tiny office so crammed with computers and measuring devices as to leave hardly any room for the two of them. Not that Pirandello seemed to mind the enforced proximity; he was a handsome, dark man in his early forties, and despite the gold ring on his wedding-finger, he had an attractively flirtatious manner.

'It's like waiting for the end of the world, no?' he

smiled, passing her a cup of outrageously strong black coffee. His window commanded an imposing view of Etna, and he caught her anxious glance at the tranquil white bulk. 'We are in no immediate danger here, I assure you.' He sat down, hitched up one immaculate trouser-crease, and crossed his legs elegantly. 'Even if Etna were to erupt right now, we would have at least three hours' grace to get ourselves and our equipment down to safety. Most of the villagers have already gone to stay with relatives elsewhere, or in hotels booked for them by the local government.'

'I'll believe you,' she smiled, still feeling anxious. His office was hung with photographs of previous eruptions, and she glanced uneasily at spectacular exposures of scarlet and yellow fountains rocketing thousands of feet into the air. 'Though I wouldn't change jobs with you, Dr Pirandello. Does all this equipment give you any idea of when the eruption's likely to take place?'

'Alas!' The corners of his mouth and eyes turned down in mock-tragedy. 'That is an impossible question, Signorina Jordan. Earthquakes and volcanoes are not predictable, regular occurrences like comets. There are too many factors involved, huge, uncomputable stresses deep in the earth.' He pointed to a needle that was registering a spidery black scrawl across graph-paper. 'As you can see, there are vibrations the whole time now. It's been that way for two weeks.' As Louise watched it, the needle swayed across the paper, drawing jagged peaks, and clicking noises came from other machines in the little office. Now she could feel it, a distant rumbling under her feet, as though a huge subway train were passing by unimaginably deep in the ground. She toyed with the idea of mentioning the 'gypsy gift' that Bruno was so sure she had, of being able to foretell quakes—and then decided not to. Somehow it seemed silly in the face of all this technology! 'The temperature of the cone,' Pirandello went on conversationally, 'is also rising steadily.'

'What does that mean?' Louise asked nervously, scribbling in her pad.

'It means that the magma—the molten lava—is slowly rising up the throat of Etna.'

'Then the eruption must be imminent?' she demanded, glancing from the complicated array of machines to the scientist's face.

'"Imminent" is a relative term,' he smiled, crow's feet spreading round his eyes. 'In geological terms, the eruption is due at any time now. So is the great earthquake that will one day disintegrate Los Angeles and half of California. But there's no way of pinpointing the event. Many scientists are working on ingenious ways of predicting these things——' He shrugged. 'Myself, I do not believe that this is possible.'

She nodded, writing fast.

The interview lasted an hour or so longer. She asked him as much about the monitoring equipment and the mountain as she thought might be useful, then took several photographs of Pirandello with the seismographs and spectroscopes and tiltmeters that were the tools of his trade. It was beginning to look as though she might be able to make a good filler article about the scientists who risked their lives on the slopes of Etna in the name of human knowledge. Absently, her mind drifted back to Taormina, and she found herself wondering whether Bruno had read her article yet. She recoiled from the thought hastily.

Dr Pirandello showed her round the rest of the

station, introducing her to some of the personnel. Many, like Dr Pirandello himself, had been involved in several previous eruptions, and had hair-raising stories to tell. All knew people who had died while working on Etna or on other volcanoes. Afterwards, he walked her to her car, obviously pleased to have had the distraction of her visit. Adrano was a strangely deserted place, a kind of ghost town, the peace and solitude of the streets in strange contrast to the titanic violence that would soon be tearing this little world apart. The villagers had been praying, Pirandello informed her, that their village would be spared, as it had been for the past fifty years. He himself felt in his scientific bones that this eruption would be bigger than normal, and might well damage the town seriously.

'However,' he said as they reached the Alfa, 'I'm sure you've had enough of Etna and her moods by now. I must confess that it's been a great pleasure to talk to such a——' He hesitated. 'Such a *feminine* woman. Journalists—especially women journalists—tend to be rather hard people, in my experience. But then, that's the trend these days, isn't it? Everyone out for themselves, broken marriages, empty relationships. Everyone's too liberated to be happy any more.'

'You blame it all on Women's Lib?' she smiled, unlocking her door.

'Not just on Women's Lib. On all Lib in general.' He grinned, showing good, even teeth. 'Moral Lib and religious Lib and sexual Lib—and all the other Libs that just mean Libido, not Liberation. You're different—you're a real woman, gentle and alluring. You don't force your way, you're not trying to be masculine the whole time. It's very refreshing.'

With a pang of pity for Pirandello, Louise wondered what sort of person Mrs Pirandello was.

'Thank you for talking to me,' she said gently. 'I'm sure your time is precious.' He shook hands with her, and waved until the Alfa was out of sight.

It was a relief to be driving away from Etna's rather forbidding presence. Ten minutes later she was at Giarre, a small town on the sea, some eight miles from the towering volcano. She glanced at the ominous cone in her rearview mirror. Giarre wasn't exactly a safe spot, she smiled wryly to herself, having been obliterated by Etna countless times in its ancient history—but she was dying to read the copy of *Women Today* that had arrived in the morning's post. And if Etna did erupt while she was reading, she'd at least have a flying start! She stopped and bought a loaf of crusty Sicilian bread and some sliced local salami, parked the Alfa overlooking the sea, and took out the glossy magazine. The portrait on the cover was stunning. She looked at the moody, brilliant photograph and remembered that first meeting with a secret inner smile. The scarlet border they'd given the photograph made it all the more dramatic, and the storyline read simply, *'Bruno Xavier—an intimate portrait by Louise Jordan.'* It was the first time her name had ever appeared on the cover, and she couldn't keep back the thrill of pride, despite everything. If only her father were alive to see this! Her mother, anyway, would be thrilled to bits.

They'd printed three full-page colour prints with the text, one showing Bruno's magnificent, near-naked body as he relaxed in the stern of the launch just after the dive, looking like a Greek sea-god newly risen from the waves, the sparkling Mediterranean behind him.

Facing was a sensitive, close-up portrait taken on the beach at Naxos, the late afternoon sun making his superbly handsome, masculine face seem luminous. There were four or five smaller photographs, two in black and white. The fine hairs on her arms prickled as she studied the brilliantly-organised lay-out, realising that it was the first time she'd seen the Naxos shots. They were beautiful. Beautiful because he was beautiful, because it had been a beautiful day, a beautiful feeling . . .

Chewing her impromptu sandwich excitedly, she read the article through again. The sub-editors had barely touched it, and again she was conscious of the profound affection and respect that was evident in her writing. If she'd been really self-aware when she'd first read through it, she'd have known that she was already falling hopelessly in love with her subject.

She grinned wryly as she saw the highlighted note at the end—*Next: The Man and The Myth—Louise Jordan will be continuing her intimate study of Bruno Xavier's life in subsequent editions of Women Today.* That was unmistakable Percy Widows, a direct attempt to blackmail her into getting more material. Subsequent editions? The way things were going, Louise Jordan would be lucky to escape from Bruno's anger alive!

Was Sophie right, she wondered? *Would* he object to this article? Except in that it was a breach of confidence, surely he could only see the love that lay behind it?

CHAPTER SIX

THURSDAY dawned brilliantly sunny and hot. She knew Bruno was going to be in Palermo today, doing some business with a local bank in which he had an interest. He'd asked her to go with him, but she'd known that she'd only be in his way, and she'd elected to stay in Taormina. She was glad of that decision now. Waiting for him to find out what she'd done was rather like waiting for Etna to erupt.

Nevertheless, she missed him badly, and spent the day in Taormina's library, buried in musty facts and figures, trying to fool herself that she was doing worthwhile research on Etna, and trying not to think about the other things on her mind.

She also avoided Sophie and the others, not feeling in the mood for company. Dinner was lonely, and she went to bed at nine-thirty that evening—ridiculously early, but she was feeling in need of comfort. She was almost asleep half an hour later when the tap at her door roused her. She switched on her bedside lamp, wrapped herself in her gown, and opened the door. It was Bruno. She could tell by a glance at his face that he hadn't found her article yet, and she melted into the warmth of his arms, hugging him with almost frantic need.

'Hey, hey,' he said softly, his breath warm in her hair. 'What's all this?' He closed the door behind them, and led her back to bed, laying her down on the coverlet. She stared up at him with blurred eyes as he stroked her hair gently away from her face. 'In bed at this hour?' he smiled.

'I—I felt a bit tired and ill.'

'Again?' He laid his hand on her forehead. 'You are a bit hot. And pale. Maybe you're coming down with summer flu.'

'Oh, it's nothing.' She nestled her cheek against his hand, feeling very melancholy, and very much in love with him. The concern on his face was like balm to her. 'It's—just one of those female things.'

'Ah. One of those female things.' He bent smilingly to kiss her mouth. 'Then you'd better get back under the blankets, *piccolina*.'

'Not yet,' she pleaded, sitting up. 'Just hold me for a minute.' He let her curl up in the sanctuary of his arms, pulling her close. He smelled of cigars and money and big city affairs. 'How was your trip to Palermo?'

'Good, but tiring.' He rested his cheek against the top of her head. 'That town's full of crooks. I only got back ten minutes ago. Your day?'

'Rotten,' she confessed. 'I missed you.'

'And I missed you.' He reached into his pocket, and dropped something into her lap. 'I've brought you a little present.'

'Bruno! I wish you hadn't.' She fumbled the little leather box open, feeling utterly miserable. On the silk lining inside was a glittering bee. Diamonds set in gold. Louise had to bite her lip to stop it trembling. It was such a lovely gift, and she didn't want to spoil it by crying now! He tilted her chin up, and looked into her face with concern in his deep grey eyes.

'Louise! What is it?'

'You shouldn't have bought me this.' She stared helplessly at the sparkling thing. It was exquisitely made, the diamonds blazing with icy fire. 'God knows I don't deserve it!'

'It's a very small bee,' he said gently. He took it from her, and pinned it on the silk of her nightgown. 'There. A distant relation.' She flung her arms round his neck, and hugged him. She'd never met anyone as generous or as thoughtful as him.

'No one ever bought me diamonds in my life,' she said indistinctly. 'It's so beautiful. Thank you, Bruno . . .'

He stroked her hair in silence while she fought down her inclination to cry. At last she sat up and looked down at the brooch with a shaky little laugh.

'You make me feel like a schoolgirl, Bruno!'

'But you are no longer a schoolgirl,' he smiled, his eyes drifting to the swell of her breasts against the silk.

She closed her eyes helplessly, drugged by the sensuality, the hint of passion in his eyes.

He kissed her softly, his hands drawing her close to him, stroking the slim shape of her body under the delicate material. Their tongues met, touched, caressed with a heart-stopping passion that made them both draw back, shuddering, to stare into one another's eyes.

There was so much promise in what they had, so much wonder, that Louise's eyes were suddenly wet with the tears she'd been fighting back all day.

'Don't cry,' he said in surprise. 'What's wrong?'

'This is all too perfect to be true,' she whispered. 'I'm so afraid it'll just vanish all of a sudden, like a dream!'

'Silly girl,' he smiled. 'No dream was ever as sweet as this.' He pulled the coverlet aside, and helped her slide herself back into bed. 'I'm not going to keep you up any longer, my love. You need sleep. Will you promise me to think about something?'

'What?' she asked.

'When your precious eruption has finally taken place, and you've got your fabulous pictures—will you come away with me?'

'Where to?' she whispered, staring into the dark pools of his eyes.

'Switzerland. I've got a summer cottage in a village called Abondance. It's very beautiful there. I bought it once in a fit of madness, and I've hardly ever been back. I'd like to take you there.' His smile caressed her heart. 'You'll have to ask for at least six weeks' leave from work. Up there among the mountains, in the silence and the peace, we'll have no distractions, no volcanoes or journalists to come between us. We'll have every second of every day to just get to know each other, inside and out. We'll see whether we really fit— heart to heart. Find out what this wonderful thing we have really is. And then we'll take the rest of our lives from there. Does that sound like a sensible arrangement?'

'No,' she said in a shaky voice. 'But a wonderful one.' She'd never felt so full, never felt so close to anyone, so aware of the potential beauty of life—and the potential sorrow. Would he still want to take her to Abondance when he knew what she'd done?

'Good.' He reached out and switched off the light. 'You can give me your answer in the next few days. Go to sleep now.' The caress of his hand on her forehead was hypnotically soothing, and her eyes closed of their own accord. Worry, sadness, joy and love were all lying heavy on her lids. Like a child, she felt herself floating swiftly down the river of sleep.

She didn't even hear the door close behind him a few minutes later. But in the darkness her lashes were wet.

And then she didn't see or hear from Bruno for three days.

She'd been expecting him to ring the next morning, Friday, to at least see how she was. He didn't. She called *Merope* on the ship-to-shore on Friday night, but there was no reply.

She was too afraid to go down there herself and see him. Saturday was a desert. She spent the week-end in steadily increasing nervous misery, waiting for him to contact her. By Sunday night, when he still hadn't done so, she knew that something had gone horribly wrong, and not all Sophie's reassurances over dinner were of any comfort. Why this cruel silence after the marvellous intimacy of Thursday night—unless he'd seen the article?

Unless everything between them was now over for ever?

She had an aching foreboding that wouldn't let her sleep the whole night.

She screwed up the last of her courage to telephone Bruno at ten on Monday morning. The voice that answered the ship-to-shore call was strange to her.

'*Qui parla il secondo. Desidera?*'

Louise blinked. *Il secondo?* The mate, she guessed. She struggled with her schoolgirl Italian, trying to find out where Bruno was. All the man knew was that he was ashore. No, he couldn't tell her where. No, there was no message for her.

Profoundly depressed, she replaced the receiver. Where was he?

The day ground past with agonising slowness. She scarcely dared to leave the hotel in case he rang her, or called by, and she spent most of her time sitting on her tiny balcony, staring at Etna in the distance, and trying to think her problems out. Sophie arrived just before sunset, seeing by a glance at Louise's face how things were.

'Trust in lady Venus,' she advised, joining Louise on the balcony to watch the glorious colours in the sky. 'She finds a way through all her subjects' perils.' They'd been sitting talking in the twilight for an hour when David Lomax arrived, carrying a copy of *Women Today*.

'Well done,' he said quietly, kissing Louise on the cheek, 'this is brilliant, Lou. Quite remarkable for someone as young as you—if you'll pardon me.'

'Exactly what I said,' Sophie smiled as Louise murmured thanks. 'Come and join us,' she invited, playing hostess for Louise. 'What about a Martini or something?'

'I'll call room service,' Louise said absently, pulling up a chair for David, and going to the telephone.

'It's quite the most sensitive account of Xavier I've ever read,' David went on, watching her affectionately through the open French door. 'It's made me see the man in a completely new light—and I'm a cynic! What does he think of it?'

'I don't know,' Louise said tautly, putting down the telephone.

David's eyebrows rose. 'He hasn't told you?'

'I haven't seen him for three days,' she said wryly. She came out into the cool night air. 'He seems to have disappeared off the face of the earth.'

'He's in the Casino right now,' David said, looking from Louise to Sophie.

'In the Casino?' Louise echoed.

'Yes. I thought you and he were—well, lovebirds. You didn't know where he was?'

'No,' Louise replied blankly, 'I didn't.'

'Well, I met Christine Sharpe in the foyer downstairs. She'd just come from the Casino. Her husband's the editor of *Impact* magazine, you know? They're staying in the Presidential suite upstairs. Rich people.' Louise nodded impatiently. She'd seen and smiled at the Sharpes several times without ever getting into conversation with them. 'Anyway,' he went on, 'Chris told me that Bruno's in the Casino now, gambling heavily.' Louise's heart sank. It didn't sound good. 'Have you had some kind of bust-up with him?' David asked, noting her unhappy expression.

'You must go to him,' Sophie said impulsively, 'right now!'

'Yes,' Louise said in a dull voice. 'But I haven't anything to wear.' She sat down numbly. 'Only casual things.'

'You want to go to the Casino—to see Bruno?' David asked, half-grasping the situation. 'That's no problem— I'll ask Chris Sharpe to lend you a dress. She's bound to have loads of beautiful things, and she's about your size—a little slimmer, maybe.'

'Oh! Would you?' Louise asked nervously.

'Sure.' David went to the telephone, and asked to be connected to the Sharpes' suite. While he was waiting, he glanced at Louise with wise eyes. 'Bruno wasn't exactly anticipating this article, right?' She nodded unhappily. David sucked his teeth. 'That could have been a bad mistake, Lou. The man's just about allergic to newsprint right now. Hullo, Carl? David Lomax here. Could I speak to Christine for a second, please?'

Half an hour later, praying he hadn't left, Louise was climbing out of her taxi in front of the Casino, wearing the dress Chris Sharpe had loaned her. As she ran up the stairs, the black silk whispering round her legs, the words she was going to say to him tumbled around crazily in her mind. For the first time in Sicily, she'd had to leave her bulky bagful of cameras behind, carrying only a simple white sharkskin purse that Sophie had lent her to go with the dress. Sophie had also looped a long, white silk scarf round her neck, which added a soft, feminine touch. Borrowed robes, she thought with a touch of bitterness. Chris had been both practical and kind; the black silk dress with its off-the-shoulder ruffles and sheer, figure-hugging Paris lines was beautiful. It had a sophistication Louise could never have afforded, would probably never have thought of buying. She didn't feel sophisticated in it, though. Her mind felt like the inside of a spin-dryer.

She'd pinned the diamond bee over her left breast.

At the *cassa* she bought twenty thousand lire's worth of plaques, the bare minimum required for entrance. Clutching the smooth tortoiseshell lozenges, she walked slowly into the noise and glitter of the Casino.

The tables were crowded, noisy. The huge modern chandeliers above gleamed on diamonds and satin and velvet, on the polished walnut and green baize of the tables, on the restless crowds laughing and chattering and losing money. Louise made her way through the throng, searching for a sign of Bruno in the vast suite of rooms. He was not at the endless bridge and poker tables, or among the excited crowd at *chemin de fer*. The whirr of the roulette wheel and the incessant slap of cards rose above the noise of conversation that was punctuated by the croupiers' monotonous and time-honoured instructions—*'Faites vos jeux, Mesdames et Messieurs'*. A tall, handsome Arab, rising from the busy roulette table to a round of applause, and with an armful of scarlet 100,000 lire plaques, offered her his chair.

'It has been a lucky seat for me, *madame*,' he assured her, 'have a try!'

She shook her head with a tight smile, and slipped past him, searching the faces with a growing lump in her throat. Then her stomach twisted inside her as she recognised Bruno.

He was sitting at the *baccarat* table, a formidably handsome figure in black dinner-jacket and black bow-tie, his bronzed face broodingly shadowed by the overhead light. She stopped dead in her tracks, watching him with her heart in her mouth. He hadn't noticed her among the crowd yet. A carelessly-scattered pile of red plaques lay beside the cards in front of him, and his long fingers were toying with the stem of a brandy-glass, his eyes hooded as he waited for the other gamblers to make their decisions.

The blonde standing behind him had her thigh intimately pressed against his arm, one red-nailed hand caressing his shoulder. Pain made Louise almost gasp out loud. There was not the slightest doubt in her mind now that he'd seen her article. After the intimacy they'd shared, the days in the sun, how could he have picked up a creature like that—unless his intention was simply to lash back at her? He knew how to hurt. Very well. She walked towards the table on legs that felt ready to buckle, wondering what in God's name she could say to him.

The croupier reached out with his slender wooden paddle, and expertly flipped Bruno's cards over. King of spades, Ace of spades.

'*Banco,*' the French croupier intoned calmly among gasps and applause. His assistant shovelled another huge pile of plaques across the baize to Bruno, whose bored expression remained unchanged, though the woman beside him kissed his cheek with over-brilliant delight. The croupier leaned forward respectfully. 'Will you accept the bank, Monsieur Xavier?'

He shrugged indifferently. 'Very well.'

As the croupier tore the cellophane off a new pack of cards, Bruno drew a panatella from his pocket and the blonde leaned forward to light it for him, whispering something into his ear. He shrugged again, exhaling. His formidable natural presence seemed to dominate the whole table despite his barely-concealed boredom. More than one wistful female gaze was on him as he waited for the pack. Through the cloud of cigar-smoke, his eyes suddenly lifted, swift as rapiers, to meet Louise's across the crowded table.

The arctic hostility in them rocked her like a slap across the mouth. The dark pupils widened for a second. Then, with a panther's lazy cruelty, the grey eyes dropped to assess her figure in the elegant black dress, and flicked indifferently past her to some other woman. As though he'd never seen her in his life before. In that moment, Louise felt as though he'd fired a bullet into her heart, and she raised her hand numbly to her breast as though there really was a physical wound there.

The croupier passed the deck over to him. He nodded thanks, draining his brandy-glass, then shuffled the pack in one efficient movement, and began flicking the cards across the table.

The blonde's eyes stayed carefully on Louise, as though she'd guessed, with a hustler's razor instincts, that there was some unspoken tension between the honey-tanned brunette with blurred green eyes and the big man beside her.

The middle-aged woman sitting just in front of Louise pushed her chair back and rose to go, clutching a multicoloured handful of plaques. Feeling as though her legs were going to give way, Louise slid into the chair she'd just vacated, opposite Bruno. His eyes met hers, hard and flat.

'New card?' he asked, his deep voice harsh.

'I—I beg your pardon?' she stammered in confusion, tugging nervously at the silk scarf round her throat. The man beside her, a white-moustached riverboat gambler type, leaned closer with a friendly smile.

'Table rules,' he informed her in a Tennessee accent. 'You can either take over the other lady's card, or ask for a new deal.'

She looked from Bruno's steel-grey eyes to the card lying face-down in front of her.

'Oh—I'll—I'll take this card, thank you.'

'As you wish,' Bruno shrugged, tapping the deck on the baize. 'Do you wish to bet?'

Colour flooded into her cheeks as she realised she barely remembered how to play. She picked up the card. Two of clubs. Remembering dimly that this was a good start, she pushed one of her tortoiseshell plaques on to the card, and sat back shakily. Bruno was dealing cards again. Another full brandy-glass had materialised at his side, and she guessed that he'd been drinking heavily this evening. And, judging by the pile at his side, winning heavily, too. She had to speak to him, no matter how he felt. Even if it was the last thing she ever said to him, she had to say something, apologise, try to explain. Yet how could she approach him now? She'd have to wait her chance.

Her second card was a five. Bruno's eyes were on her again, chilling her. She barely noticed the others at the table, expensively-dressed people talking and laughing softly, some with the hungry eyes and pale faces of compulsive gamblers. She pushed another plaque forward, trying with crazy logic to remember whether she could make a five-card trick. Without speaking, or taking his eyes off hers, Bruno flicked another card over. She tore her eyes away to look at it. A nine. Sixteen altogether. She laid her last plaque on the pile, realising emptily that if she lost she'd have to get up and leave. An expectant hush settled on the table as the gamblers' eyes, envious, sympathetic, fearful, watched Louise's face. The fourth card was a four. The riverboat gambler leaned forward again, excitement in his whisper.

'You have to turn your cards over now if you want to try for a five-card. Otherwise stick with twenty.'

Without thinking, she laid the cards face-up on the table. There was a silence as everyone counted.

'Twenty,' Bruno said softly. The blonde was biting her painted lips, her eyes intent on Louise with a hustler's sympathy. Somebody giggled nervously. His eyes still on hers, Bruno laid out her fifth card. Ace of Diamonds.

The riverboat gambler let out a whoop of delight beside her, and the table burst into laughter and applause, even the croupier's sombre face breaking into a smile. Through the hubbub, Louise leaned forward to Bruno, her eyes pleading.

'I must talk to you,' she begged softly, her voice meant only for his ears.

There was no answer from his eyes. He slid two 50,000 lire plaques across the table towards her, and began the reshuffle, his cigar clenched between his teeth.

'Maybe the luck's going to change,' the riverboat gambler said exultantly. 'What say, Mr Xavier? Will the little lady get the bank next time?'

'I doubt it,' Bruno said casually, the authority in his face making the other's smile fade. He looked up with eyes as cold as the muzzles of two revolvers. 'Tonight I happen to be infallible.'

'How so?' a distinguished-looking woman of about fifty asked beside him, her smile deliberately sensual.

'Because, my dear Countess,' he said quietly, 'I have been unlucky in love.' He flicked the last card out. *'Faites vos jeux.'* The Countess laughed softly. She studied her card for a moment, then threw a plaque on to it, toying with the diamonds at her throat.

'That is unlike you, Bruno. With you it is usually the others who are unlucky, not so?'

'Besides,' someone else said, looking pointedly at the blonde's voluptuous cleavage, 'your ill-luck is not exactly in evidence, Signor Xavier.' There was laughter round the table. Louise bit back the wince that crossed her face, and dropped her eyes to her card. It was the Ace of Hearts. A good omen? She looked up to find Bruno stonily studying the satiny skin of her throat and shoulders. Colouring, she shuffled all her plaques on to the card. The riverboat gambler whistled, and somebody called 'Bravo!' Bruno's commanding mouth turned down infinitesimably, registering scorn. The Countess was watching Louise with an enigmatic smile.

'Such beautiful green eyes,' she murmured, almost to herself. 'Perhaps the luck is indeed going to change.' Louise sat with heavily beating heart, watching Bruno deal out the second round of cards. The game was passing like some crazy dream, unreal and distant. All she could think of was getting past that armoured reserve of Bruno's, figuring out some way of getting to him, making him give her a chance to explain. She didn't even look at her second card, something which didn't escape the riverboat gambler.

'I guess you must know something the rest of us don't,' he grinned, making his bets. Another hush settled on the table as the game began. The Countess stuck on three cards, probably an eighteen or nineteen by her satisfied expression. Two others went bust, and the riverboat gambler tried valiantly for a five-card, and drew a Queen.

'Shucks,' he said, pure Nashville, 'I guess the luck's not changing yet.' Bruno's eyes were on Louise again.

'I'll stick,' she said, her voice sounding small. He turned his own cards over, two Knaves.

'The bank pays twenty-one,' he said calmly.

The croupier flipped the Countess' cards over, expert eyes counting swiftly.

'Dix-neuf.'

'The luck certainly isn't changing yet,' she sighed as the croupier raked her chips over to Bruno. She turned an amused smile on Louise. 'We're counting on you, Miss Green Eyes,' she murmured.

The croupier leaned forward, and flipped Louise's cards. The other card was the King of Spades.

'Banco,' the croupier said in the dead silence. Again, the table erupted in delight. It had been a fantastic pair of successive wins, and the new bank had lasted barely two rounds. There was no pleasure in Louise's heart as her eyes pleaded with Bruno again.

'Will you accept the bank, *mademoiselle?*' the croupier asked, shovelling scarlet plaques her way.

She hesitated, tugging at her scarf restlessly. 'Can I pass it back to the house?'

'Of course, *mademoiselle*,' the croupier bowed, snapping his fingers for a new pack.

'You should have kept the bank,' the riverboat gambler reproved. 'Having the bank gives you a real edge.'

'So, *mademoiselle*,' the Countess said softly, 'you have changed the luck after all.'

'Yeah,' riverboat agreed, winking at Bruno's grim expression. 'Your theory didn't seem to apply, Mr Xavier!'

'Or perhaps,' Louise said quietly, 'Signor Xavier was not so unlucky at love as he imagined.' The blonde pressed against Bruno with feline grace, obviously wanting him to leave now.

'Perhaps you are right,' Bruno grated, addressing Louise directly. 'In which case, *mademoiselle*, I should console myself with having had a fortunate escape.'

'And you,' someone said to Louise from further up the table, 'must be the one who has been unluckiest of all.'

'Oh,' the Countess smiled, eyeing Louise's suddenly-huge pile of plaques, 'money is a great consolation, is it not, *mademoiselle*?'

'I have never found it so,' Louise said quietly, her eyes still pleading with Bruno. The anger in his face was like the tension before an electric storm, felt and dreaded, rather than seen. 'Money is not happiness.'

'Hear, hear,' riverboat chuckled.

'You surprise me,' Bruno said silkily, leaning back to study Louise as though she was a botanical specimen under the microscope. 'For I've known women who would sell their bodies and their souls for money. There are even those, *mademoiselle*,' he said, his voice becoming deadly soft, 'who, for money, will sell the souls of others.'

Louise's tan faded to pearly white, and her voice was barely a whisper in the hush that was falling around the table.

'That would be a terrible crime, signor. Can you be so sure that you have not misjudged some of these— women?'

'Misjudged?' His smile was colder than the edge of a scimitar. 'I think not.'

'Come come, Bruno,' the Countess said, toying with the brilliants in her necklace, 'I hope you are not condemning the whole female sex?'

'I was not speaking in such general terms,' Bruno said, turning to her with a kind of lethal grace. 'There was a time when I thought I had found an exception. A woman different from the rest, sweet and true.' He looked at the card which the croupier had just flicked in front of him, and tossed a plaque on to it. 'But that was in another country. And besides, the bitch is dead.' Complete and appalled silence fell on the table, and Louise's soul felt as though it would wither inside her, her whole being blasted by the utter hostility and indifference in his manner. Aware of the hush, Bruno glanced up with a velvety smile. 'I meant nothing personal, my friends. I simply quoting from Ben Jonson.'

'Ben Jonson, eh?' the riverboat gambler said nervously. 'He must have been quite a guy.' The Countess' quick gaze caught the sheen of tears in Louise's eyes.

'Bruno,' she said in a low voice, 'à volte tu sei trop cruele.'

'Cruelty, my dear Countess, is the way of the world.' He counted his chips, dropped a few in his pocket, and passed the rest over to the croupier's assistant, who wrote out a note in return. He checked it carelessly and tucked it into his wallet. Then he crushed out his cigar, and rose with the fluid grace Louise knew so well, his arm sliding possessively round the giggling blonde's waist. 'I'm afraid I must leave you, *mes amis.*' He didn't even glance at Louise, sitting with breaking heart in her chair, as he turned away. 'Goodnight.'

'What the hell was all that about?' someone asked as he walked away.

'Mesdames et Messieurs,' the croupier pleaded in the heavy silence, *'faites vos jeux*—the game must go on.'

Suddenly, something seemed to snap inside Louise— an inner scream of *No!* No to his cruelty, no to the way Fate had tossed out the cards in the game of her life, no to the destruction of her happiness for ever.

She rose, her green eyes blazing, and went after him. *'Mademoiselle!'* the croupier called after her, 'you have forgotten your *jetons*——' She was deaf to his entreaty, or the buzz of conversation that arose behind her. She caught up with them at the *roulette* table, and grasped at Bruno's arm, thrusting herself in their way.

'You've got to listen to me,' she panted, staring up at him as though her life depended on it, and ignoring the astonished expression on the blonde's painted face. 'You *must* give me a chance to apologise, Bruno——'

' "Must"?' He shook her hand off contemptuously. '*Must* is not a word to use to me, Louise.'

'It wasn't the way you think,' she said desperately. 'I didn't set out to exploit you, I swear I didn't!'

A babble of conversation and laughter from the nearby *roulette* table intervened, and the blonde's expression hardened.

'Perhaps, *caro,*' she said, clinging to Bruno's arm

with overdone affection, 'your lady-friend has had a little too much to drink, yes?'

'Bruno,' Louise pleaded, 'after everything we had—don't you at least owe me a hearing? You can't believe that I set out to deceive you——'

'Why not?' he said icily. 'It's been done before. Not with as much finesse, I admit—but just as effectively for being a little cruder. As for what we had——' His eyes blazed. 'I am not such an idiot as to imagine that any of it was real.'

'*Andiamo, caro,*' the blonde urged, wanting him to go.

'You think I'm just like Laura Ackermann—but I'm not.' She shook her head, eyes bright with unshed tears. 'I'm not, I swear it.'

'You want the second instalment, is that it?' Disdain curled his passionate mouth. 'Go and find another fool, Louise. The sight of you makes me sick.'

'Oh, my love,' Louise said, close to despair, 'I didn't think you'd be this hurt, I didn't—I wrote that article because I cared for you, because I wanted to tell the whole world about you——'

'*You* wanted!' Grey fury exploded in his eyes, acrid, lethal. The blonde yelped in protest as he thrust her away and took Louise's chin in a frighteningly tight grip. 'You selfish little——' He bit the word off, somehow making his anger all the more painful to her. 'A woman who had the slightest grain of feeling could never have dreamed of doing what you did. But you don't have feelings, do you Louise? Except for money!'

'Oh Bruno,' she said, the silky sheen of her lips trembling uncontrollably, 'you're so wrong. You must believe me! I didn't know when I started this how very much I would come to love you——'

He released her chin with a harsh laugh, the mark of his fingers pale against the honey. 'You soil words like "love" on your lips, woman.'

'Caro.' The blonde laid her hand on his arm, her expression anxious. 'It is late——'

'Vattene,' he growled at her, turning back to Louise as though he would have taken pleasure in striking her. 'You've done to me what not even Laura could—you found your way into my very heart, and then betrayed me. I've been such a fool, such a damned fool that it amazes me when I look back.' He shook his head bitterly. 'You must have found it all so easy, Louise. God, how you must have laughed!'

'Am I laughing now?' she asked huskily, tears brimming on her long lashes.

'I am no longer impressed by actresses' tricks,' he sneered. 'Trembling lips, wet eyes, the catch in the voice—it's all false. False as the way you kissed me, false as the way you gasped in my arms.'

'No,' she pleaded, 'none of that is false. You mean more to me than anyone else in the world, more than life itself——'

'And yet you sold me?' he ridiculed, eyebrows arching in a cruel parody of surprise. 'The female heart must be a strange place, in truth.' He grinned savagely. 'Like a tiger's maw, which demands fresh blood daily.'

'I didn't sell you,' she said, shaking her head, willing him to believe her. 'I didn't write to make money—look at that article again, and see how much I care for you!'

People had begun to stare at them, and the blonde plucked ineffectually at Bruno's sleeve. A nervous manager was standing by, wringing his gloved hands with a shaky smile, obviously afraid of an explosive public scene involving this valued and famous client.

'Your caring isn't worth a curse,' Bruno replied, his face a cynical mask of bronze.

'Please,' she said, fighting back the tears that threatened to choke her words, 'let me make it up to you in some way! For the love of God, Bruno, let me apologise somehow!'

His eyes narrowed, smoky and dangerous. 'What did you have in mind?'

'I'd do anything,' she said unevenly, pushing her dark, glossy hair away from her face with trembling fingers. 'Anything that would prove to you how sorry I am—I swear it——'

A cruel speculation glittered in his smile. He stepped back, one fist on his hip, dark eyes dropping to study her figure, the sweet curves that were hinted at under the sheer black dress. 'Anything?' She nodded silently, frightened by the wicked slant of his mouth, the velvety way his anger had changed course suddenly. 'There is only one thing I want from you, Louise.' Irony smouldered in his eyes, merciless, mocking. 'You enriched yourself by using me. That was a whore's payment. What else can you offer in return except a whore's services?'

The colour drained from her cheeks abruptly. 'I—I don't understand you, Bruno. What do you mean?'

'I mean this body of yours.' He reached out to trail his knuckles down the satin of her throat, his smile pitiless. The touch made her shut her eyes helplessly, oblivious of the blonde's angry exclamation. 'You must be an expert at pleasing men,' he said, controlled hatred rough in his deep voice. 'It is part of your stock-in-trade, not so? That is the payment I demand, Louise. Please me tonight.'

'Bruno——' she gasped, unable to believe what he

was saying, realising with shock that he thought her little better than a courtesan.

'How well you counterfeit shock,' he sneered. 'You must have a thousand emotions at your fingertips, like Sarah Bernhardt herself!'

'You don't mean what you've just asked,' she faltered, her voice almost a plea.

'I mean exactly what I say,' he said curtly, the velvet becoming steel again. 'Come with me to *Merope* tonight—or get out of my life for ever.'

'Tell me there's a little tenderness in what you ask,' she whispered, hypnotised by the cruel eyes, 'even an ounce——'

'There's none at all,' he said ruthlessly. 'All my illusions died today, Louise. What I mean is pure, physical lust.' His smile was dark, Satanic. 'My only regret is that I haven't been paid in full.'

'This isn't you talking,' she faltered. 'It can't be—it's someone else, some stranger I've never seen before——'

He turned away, boredom curling his lip. 'Then goodbye, little journalist.' He took the blonde's hand. *'Andiàmo.'*

'No!' Louise gasped, unable to bear seeing him go. He turned to her indifferently.

'What is it?'

'I——' She choked down tears. 'I'll come.'

'Too late,' he mocked. 'I have chosen my partner for the night.'

'Please,' she whispered, shame closing her eyes. The simple truth was that she couldn't bear to let him walk away. Any more than she could have let her heart stop beating. 'Please don't go.'

'Let me understand you properly,' he purred, silky

enjoyment in his smile. 'You're begging to spend the night with me?'

'*Caro*,' the blonde urged in a low hiss, 'enough of this game. Let's go!'

'Answer my question,' he said, ignoring her, his eyes dark, remorseless on Louise's face.

Humiliation scalded her cheeks, drying the tears on her lashes and all feeling in her heart.

'Yes,' she whispered, unable to meet that dreadful triumph in his gaze. She was committed now, irrevocably.

'Even though you fully understand,' he went on in a panther's purr, 'that tomorrow morning, having used your body, I will throw you out of my bed and tell you never to come near me again?'

She parted heavy lids to look into his face with eyes that seemed drugged by his cruelty, as though this were some nightmare she couldn't escape from, a wheel of flame on which she was inexorably bound.

'Yes.' Her lips formed the word, but no sound came out.

'Excellent,' he said, coals of triumph igniting in his eyes. 'Then let us go at once.' He turned to the waiting blonde, three 50,000 lire plaques in his fingers.

'*Tieni.*' The blonde opened her crimson lips to protest, caught sight of the expression on his eyes, and smiled brightly. She took the chips, shot Louise a glance of pure malice, and walked away with an exaggerated swing of the hips.

Louise felt as though she was about to faint, the tension of the past few minutes dizzying her mind. Utterly indifferent to her glazed expression, Bruno took her arm in steel fingers, and walked her calmly through the glittering, unnoticing throng.

CHAPTER SEVEN

STILL in a kind of nightmare, she walked with him down into the underground car park. 'Where are you taking me?' she asked, almost afraid of him in this terrible mood.

'To my new plaything,' he said shortly. She glanced up into his face dazedly. Was he drunk? She'd seen him gulp down two large brandies at least, and his savage behaviour was probably due at least partly to its effect in his blood.

'You aren't going to drive down to *Mazzaró* are you?' she queried timidly, thinking of the hairpin bends on the long drive down.

'Are your morals reasserting themselves?' he asked contemptuously.

'I don't want you to drive if——' She bit the words off, not wanting to anger him further.

'If I'm drunk?' he said, his deep voice harshly amused. 'Here—my new toy.' She stared at the car blankly, ten feet of black, sleek, gleaming death under the floodlights.

'Bruno!'

'It's a Maserati,' he said drily, his eyes watching her expression with cynical amusement. 'I picked it up in Catánia this morning. Don't you think it rather goes with the image, my dear Louise?'

'You don't need an image,' she said, her heart thumping as she looked at the cruel, gleaming shape of the sportscar. 'You never have done. Bruno, let's take a taxi down——'

He flung the door open, his expression brutal. 'Get in.'

She obeyed, as afraid as though she were embracing her own death, and buckled her seat belt as he climbed in beside her, and slid the key into the ignition.

'This is a joke,' she begged him, 'isn't it?'

'I am not in a joking mood,' he said silkily. 'Have you changed your mind? Because if you have, I can always find my blonde friend—or a dozen like her.'

She didn't answer, but closed her eyes, her hands clenched helplessly in her lap. What was she doing here, what crazy self-punishment was she expecting to achieve? Only the slaking of Bruno's anger on her own body?

The twin exhausts boomed in the echoing garage like a gun, and he twisted the wheel, urging the car out of its bay and on to the concrete ramp that led out into the night.

'I wanted to tell you how sorry I am,' she said in a low voice. 'I wanted to tell you how much I loved you, how much I regretted having done what I did . . .'

'Please,' he said caustically, 'end the little charade, Louise. There's no one to appreciate it any more.'

'It's no charade.' She fought for the right words, clinging to the strap beside her as he swung the car through the narrow streets. She loved him so very much! If only she could show him an inkling of the depth of her feeling for him, the ache in her heart for him—'I know I was wrong to publish what you told me, Bruno. But I wasn't thinking, I was mad——'

'You were thinking clearly enough when it came to how much money it was going to bring you,' he retorted.

'I know how much I've offended you,' she tried

again, 'coming so soon after what Laura Ackermann did to you——'

'Don't knock Laura,' he said with rough irony. 'She could give *you* points. At least she didn't come back to me, whining apologies after the kill.'

'I'd give anything to be able to make it better,' she said in a low voice, biting her lip.

'Better?' He laughed with genuine amusement. 'You don't imagine that I'm hurt any more?' He glanced at her pale face, and swung the powerful car on to the *autostrada*, accelerating hard. 'You flatter yourself. I simply need a partner for the night—and my little blonde friend was painfully empty-headed.'

'Bruno,' she said, her voice barely audible above the engine's snarl, 'I've never—I've never been with a man before——'

'D'you expect me to believe that?' he drawled disdainfully, shifting gear smoothly, 'coming from a pathological liar like you?' They were accelerating fast into a sharp bend, the white headlights stabbing off the edge of the road into nothingness. 'Sex is a part of your equipment, not so, Louise? Like the tape-recorder you must have had in that bulky bag. Or all those expensive cameras. Simply a way of opening the mouths of fools.'

'You are cruel!' That he should think she was sexually callous, a woman who used her body to get her own way, somehow hurt more than anything else.

'Because I speak the truth?'

The first of the hairpin bends came up, and the Maserati surged into the tight corner with a scream of skidding rubber, thrusting Louise back against the cream hide of the seats.

'For God's sake,' she gasped, 'you're driving too fast!' He didn't answer, spinning the wheel in expert hands as the road ran along the clifftop, swinging the car ruthlessly into the next corner.

'We've been so much to each other,' she went on, trying not to look at the road that rushed terrifyingly fast under their wheels. 'Can you really want to do this to me, Bruno?'

'You mean make love to you?' He shrugged callously. 'Wasn't that your contingency plan, in any case? If I hadn't proved so stupidly co-operative with you, would you not have offered me your body, too?'

'No,' she said quietly. 'Not like this.'

'Why "not like this"?' he laughed roughly. The brakes screamed again as he accelerated into another hairpin bend, the luminous green dial of the speedometer showing 120 kilometres. The car swung on its superb suspension, pressing Louise against the door as though with a giant hand, and she covered her eyes in real terror, unable to believe they weren't going to plummet off the winding road and into space.

He controlled the car with nerveless skill, his hands sure on the wheel as they hurtled into the next straight. Despite the speeds he kept up, the way he handled the car was too brilliantly skilful for his senses to have been much dulled by the brandy he'd drunk. A blinding blaze of headlights whipped past on the other side of the road, the only car they'd encountered.

'Because,' she went on in a trembling voice, 'when we made love, it would have been with love, and tenderness, and desire—not as a punishment!' She squeezed her eyes shut again on the next bend, wondering whether he even remotely believed what she was saying. A heavy ache had settled in her stomach. She'd never thought of herself as a particularly moral person. It certainly hadn't been any strong moral feeling that had stopped her from sleeping with other men. But the thought of making love with Bruno—having sex with him—with no feeling between them but anger, was horrifying. It appalled her that he could even contemplate hurting her like this, using the vulnerability of her love for him as a target.

And she did love him—she knew that now, deep in her heart. She would never love another man the way she loved Bruno—and beside the fear of losing him, the article, Etna, the whole of Sicily itself, had no more importance than a dream. She kept silent during the terrifying drive down, still half-believing at the back of her mind that he would relent, would see how much he'd already hurt her, and might begin to forgive her. As they approached the beach at Mazzaró she looked out of the windscreen at the red glow in the distance that was Etna. And you still remain silent, she thought with deep sadness. We humans fret and fuss and wound one another—and you keep your inscrutable fires, brooding till your time is right . . .

Mazzaró was deserted, the sea dark as wine beneath a moon that had begun to wane. He pulled the Maserati up next to the pier, and Louise was vaguely glad to be still alive as she stepped out into the night, her legs wobbly. He took her arm in the same fierce grip, and walked her along the pier to where the launch was moored, a slim white shape in the night. She picked up the hem of her dress as he helped her silently into the launch, for the first time wondering what Christine Sharpe was going to say when her exquisite black dress didn't make a reappearance the next morning.

The thought cast a deep melancholy over her mind. She was, if Bruno's ruthless anger held, on the brink of losing her innocence. Maidenhood was something she hadn't bothered much about in twenty-two years—yet now, the thought of the change that was shortly to come over her was profoundly depressing. She sat in the stern with clasped hands, staring at Bruno's elegant figure at the wheel, forbiddingly dark but for the white silk of his shirt. She'd dreamed of his love-making, dreamed of surrendering to the heat of his desire. But she could never have anticipated, in her wildest dreams, that she would do so as an act of vengeance. That he would take her virginity, not even knowing he was doing so, believing her to be as experienced as any courtesan . . .

He was silent now, taut as a sword-blade, and just as deadly. The launch surged out across the calm sea to where *Merope* lay pearled with lights under the moon, and she wondered vaguely whether this was how lost souls had felt, when Charon the dark ferryman had taken the coins from their lips, and carried them into the land of perpetual night . . .

They reached *Merope*, and Bruno tied the launch alongside the dinghy that was bobbing on the tide.

The yacht was silent. The crew would still be on leave, she remembered. They walked into the stateroom, neither speaking. He switched on the Empire lamp on the desk, and by its soft light she saw at a glance that his face was unrelenting. As cruel as the bronze mask of some warrior-king, she thought with a shudder. He picked up a crystal decanter, and splashed brandy into two glasses.

'Here,' he said indifferently, offering her one, 'this may improve your performance.'

She took the glass, remembering with a sharp pain when she had last taken a glass from him in this room. 'Bruno,' she said quietly, 'I find it hard to believe that this is really you talking.'

'Really?' he arched one dark eyebrow. 'Am I not living up to the image?'

'To the image, yes.' She drank, choking a little on the neat spirit, but grateful for its slight warming effect on her heart. 'But you're not being true to yourself—to the Bruno Xavier I know and love.'

'Again that word on your lips,' he said with a cold smile. He gulped the brandy down, then looked at her with wintry eyes. 'The real Bruno Xavier, eh? But what of yourself, my little journalist—who is the real Louise Jordan? The melting creature of a summer's afternoon— or the businesswoman who calmly sold the man who trusted her?'

She turned away from the hatred in his eyes, the temporary effect of the brandy chilled out of her veins, and stared dully down into her tumbler.

'How did you come across my article?' she asked in a low voice, '—not that it matters.'

'Not that it matters,' he echoed. 'I went to Catánia early on Friday morning to meet the director of one of my companies. I was somewhat surprised to find my own face staring back at me from half-a-dozen newsagents' windows.'

'I see,' she said softly.

'Indeed,' he said indifferently, picking up the decanter again. 'Thanks to you, *Woman Today* is receiving an international exposure which its normal fare of knitting patterns and——' His purr dripped sarcasm. '—*in-depth* news articles would scarcely warrant.'

'Have you even read my article?' she asked, turning to face him with the cold glass pressed to her cheek.

'As much of it as I could stomach,' he shrugged.

'Didn't you find it even slightly appealing?' she

pleaded. 'Couldn't you tell by the way I wrote how I felt about you?'

'You stand there discussing style,' he retorted, his eyes clouded with anger. 'What the hell does it matter whether the article was well-written or not, in English, Italian, or Swahili? The simple fact remains that I told you some of the most intimate details of my life. Because I thought you were special, because I cared about you.' He walked to the window, his body tense with suppressed violence. 'Never dreaming that you would print every word, that you would use the tragedy of my parents' life and death to sell your wretched little magazine——' He stopped, staring blindly out into the night, then turned to her. 'I was a blind fool, I agree. Why I should have trusted a journalist, after Laura, is a mystery. An emotional aberration. I suppose by the shadowy morals of your profession you were more or less justified in taking advantage of a fool.' His mouth tightened. 'But you didn't have to play with my feelings as well. That was an unforgivable betrayal. And shall I tell you what hurt me most of all?'

'Yes,' she whispered.

'In that article, you quoted me word perfect. Much too perfect to have been mere memory. I realised that you must have had a tape-recorder with you that day at Naxos. Didn't you?'

'Yes,' she whispered again, her face changing colour.

'One of the miniature models, I suppose. Hidden in that bag of yours. And every time we met after that, every time we talked, or kissed, or lay in each other's arms—you were recording every word and whisper.'

'*No!*'

'And all the things I said to you, the stupid,

sentimental phrases of my infatuation—they've all been carefully recorded, have they not?'

'No, I swear it,' she said desperately. 'I did use a tape-recorder at Naxos—but I left it in the hotel after that! I only took it along in case I forgot any details——'

'Quite the little Mata Hari,' he said softly, looking as though he would relish the taste of her blood on his tongue. 'Do you expect me to believe such transparent inventions? You would have gone as far as Laura Ackermann, Louise. Much further, even, because I trusted you, and would have let you further into my secret heart. I even fooled myself that I——' He bit his lip hard. 'No doubt you would have repeated Laura's sensational success in the English-language press. Except that you—or your editor—got greedy. Impatient. And printed the first instalment right away, hoping I wouldn't see it until you'd got what you wanted——'

'That isn't true,' she burst in, close to tears. 'I wrote that article because you fascinated me. But if I'd had any idea how much you were going to resent it, I'd sooner have died——'

'Your lies make me sick,' he snarled. He jerked a drawer of the desk open, and pulled out the crimson-bordered copy of *Women Today*, flinging it at her. It fell open on the Persian rug, at the last page of her article. 'What does that mean?' he demanded bitterly, pointing at the highlighted caption at the end. She stared at it dumbly. *Next: The Man and The Myth— Louise Jordan will be continuing her intimate study of Bruno Xavier's life in subsequent editions of Women Today.*

'It means nothing,' she told him, already despairing

of ever getting past his anger now. 'It's just an empty promise—my editor was hoping I'd be able to write some more. But I never would have done——'

'And what was the next instalment to consist of?' he grated. 'Bruno Xavier in bed? Bruno Xavier's words of endearment to a woman who'd made a fool out of him?'

'You know I could never have done such a thing,' she said, shaking her head hopelessly. Her eyes were wet again, her lips trembling. He walked up to her slowly, and took her face in hands that were so gentle that she almost gave way to the grief bursting inside her.

'So beautiful,' he said, his voice husky, his eyes dark and misty. 'So beautiful that I could almost believe you—were the evidence not lying at your feet in black and white.' He kissed her cold lips, gently. 'Oh, Louise,' he said in a rough growl, 'you don't know how much you've hurt me. I would have given my heart's blood for all this not to be true, to be able to believe your sweet lies.'

'They're true,' she pleaded, the emotions of the past hours telling in her strained mouth and eyes. 'If you listened to your heart, and not to your eyes, you'd know I'm telling you the truth—you'd see how dreadfully sorry I am, how much I want to apologise——'

'Hush,' he said softly, the expression in his eyes melting her bones. The frightening stranger had vanished, and in his place was the old Bruno—*her* Bruno, the gentle lover who'd taught her heart to feel. She laid her hands over his, sensing the depth of his feeling for her like a warm river all around. There was so much tenderness for her in this powerful man, buried deep beneath his anger, so much if she could only reach it. If only he hadn't locked it away for ever.

'You must believe me, Bruno—I never meant to hurt you like this. I should have thought, I know I should have asked your permission—but I was so excited at the time. You'd walked into my life, lighting it up like the sun——'

He stepped back, disgust curling his lip again.

'Still lies, and more lies,' he said, his voice a velvety threat. The anger re-ignited like hot petrol in his smile. 'Come,' he commanded, reaching for her hand. 'Your bargain—time is wasting.'

Hopelessly, she gave him her fingers, and he led her to the doorway, and into the dark corridor beyond.

Her heart was beating like a trapped bird as he flung the double-doors open at the end of the corridor.

'Come come,' he sneered as she hesitated, 'no false modesty, surely!'

She walked through with a feeling of dread in the pit of her stomach, her mind shying away from what was to come the way a nervous horse might shy from fire. Perhaps if she just didn't think about it, if she closed her mind to it all, it might not hurt so very much——

The cabin was dramatically luxurious, dominated by the vast, wine-red bed in the centre, overhung by a dark silk canopy, spangled with tiny stars.

'This fits with the image, *n'est-ce pas?*' he said ironically, closing the doors behind him. He was still carrying his brandy glass in one hand. 'I hope you're making a note of all the details—your readers will be fascinated.'

'Please,' she said, 'stop now.'

He raised mocking eyebrows. 'Aren't you going to turn this evening's—entertainment—into a six-page article? You'd be a fool not to take full advantage, Louise.' He pointed to the white sharkskin bag she held. 'I'm sure you've got your little tape-recorder in there—haven't you?'

She shook her head silently, holding the bag out to him. He took it from her, his eyes never leaving hers, and laid it unopened on the ormolu dressing-table, beside his glass. How fluid his movements were, she thought dully, like a great cat amusing itself before the kill. The dinner-jacket he wore suited him best of all garments, its severe elegance complementing his magnificent figure, the virile lines of his body. That was how she had first seen him—but then the jacket and bow-tie had been white. Now they were black.

She fought back her panicky instinct to shrink away as he came to her, her pulses feeling as though they were jumping out of her skin.

He reached out and loosened the white silk scarf from her throat, pulling it away with agonising slowness, and letting it drift to the floor. His expression was dark, enigmatic. He touched her chin with his forefinger, then trailed it lingeringly down the curve of her throat, his eyes studying her mouth with smouldering intensity. She was trembling now, uncontrollably, trying to bite down her fear of him, the pain he was causing her.

'You're shaking, Louise,' he said in his deep, velvety voice. An ironic smile touched the corners of his mouth. 'Do I frighten you?'

'Yes,' she said, her voice catching in her dry throat.

'Why?'

'You've only touched me in tenderness before,' she faltered. 'This time it's in anger——'

'Does it hurt?' he purred, his eyes enjoying the tremor

of her lips as he caressed her cheek with silky gentleness.

'Not physically. But I'd rather you struck me, drew blood in passion—than caressed me in hatred!'

'Are you still keeping up this pretence of caring for me?' he ridiculed.

'If it's a pretence,' she said unevenly, 'then it's one I shall keep up all my life.'

'So,' he said, his smile sardonic. '*La commedia non é ancora finita.* Take off your shoes, Louise.' She hesitated, then dropped her eyes, and stepped out of the high-heeled sandals she'd been wearing, the carpet soft under her bare feet.

It was disconcerting to discover that she was suddenly three inches shorter. He towered over her now, the power of his body emphasised against her slenderness.

He reached for her shoulders, drawing her face to his. She opened her mouth to cry out, but his lips were swift and warm against her own. She stood rigid, her body still trembling in his arms. His tongue teased her lips open with easy skill, his kiss dominating her as effortlessly as though it were some game in which the rules were all on his side. Without her volition, her arms stole around his neck, her fingers shakily brushing his thick hair at first; then, as a slow fire began to uncoil inside her, she swayed towards him, her breasts brushing against his chest. Only the slap of waves against the hull disturbed the infinite silence, the deep peace of the night.

Her lips clung to his when at last he drew back, as though unwilling to be released. He pulled her close to his body, drawing her face against his shoulder, his fingers exploring the dark curls of her hair. When he spoke, his voice was low, his accent harsh beneath the velvet.

'How often I've dreamed of what we're going to do, Louise. I longed for this so many times before——' He stopped, then went on in a husky voice, '—before the fall. But in my dreams we did this for our mutual pleasure, as a sign and an act of love.'

'It can be that now,' she pleaded, deeply moved. She closed her eyes, drugged by his caress in her hair. This was why she had come here tonight—with the secret hope that their love-making itself might soften his heart. A reckless gamble that at the moment of truth, Bruno's deep-buried feelings of tenderness for her would resurface. Would it turn out that way? She clung to him, praying it would. 'Only a very little change would make it an act of love again, Bruno,' she whispered. 'It's only a state of mind which makes it hate, not love, vengeance, not worship.'

'A state of mind,' he repeated. 'So young, and yet so cynical?' He pushed her away, staring down into her open face. 'And so lovely . . .' He released her, and turned away, breaking the moment's spell. He picked up the brandy-glass, his back to her, and drank. Barefoot, feeling like a child, she watched him, wondering what was going on in his mind. He turned to her suddenly, and passed her the half-full glass. 'You won money from me tonight.'

'Did I? Oh, yes.' She smiled tiredly. 'I'd forgotten.' She gulped the fiery spirit down, wishing it would cauterise her feelings. 'I left it in the Casino when I jumped up to follow you. Was it a lot?'

'About five hundred thousand lire,' he answered, taking the empty glass from her. 'Enough for a very pretty bauble.'

He tugged his tie loose, baring his throat. It was strange to be talking almost casually like this. When was he going to claim his vengeance? 'The tide has changed. Did you feel it?'

She shook her head, his gentleness surprising her. 'I'm no good with tides and things.'

'Tell me something,' he said, pulling off his jacket, and dropping it on a chair. 'What did you want the money for? The money you'll get from that article, I mean?'

'The money?' She shook her head. 'The money meant nothing to me. It means even less now. If you want to know why I wrote that article—I can hardly remember any more. Because you were too big for me to keep to myself. I wanted to share you, show other people how beautiful life could be . . .'

'Ah, Louise,' he said bitterly, 'is the truth so hard to tell?'

'No,' she said quietly, 'just hard to believe.' They faced one another in silence, antagonists once more. Then he came to her in one stride, his fingers biting into her shoulders, his mouth claiming hers with a ruthless hunger that shook her. There was no tenderness now, only a fierce authority that tore away her defences, taking possession of her mind and body. There were no more words, no thoughts—just a blind passion that impelled them together with a current as strong as the sea. His hands slid hungrily down her back as they kissed, moulding the flare of her hips, pulling her thighs against his as though he couldn't bear even an inch of their bodies not to be touching.

She was gasping for breath, the blood pounding in her ears, when he drew back.

'Don't——' she begged him, 'please, Bruno—not like this——'

'It's too late, Louise,' he grated, his eyes glowing with the desire she could feel, furnace-hot, against her body. She dropped her head, unable to bear the intensity of that look, her dark hair tumbling over her face. He reached for the zipper at the back of her dress, and with slow deliberation, drew it down the length of her back. She shuddered at the whisper of the silk, the breath of cool air on her naked skin. There was no turning back now, no return on the tide of his passion. She didn't even try and resist as he eased Christine Sharpe's expensive black dress off her tanned shoulders, and let it slide to the floor. His fingers were surprisingly gentle as he pushed the heavy, glossy hair away from her face, and held her at arm's length, studying her slim, innocent body with dark eyes. She was wearing only simple briefs, the satin of her skin burnt-honey in the soft light, her arms clasped protectively over the cream of her breasts. His gaze seemed to scorch her skin, making her feel more naked than she had ever done before. No man had ever looked at her like this, so intimately—yet apart from the quick, shallow breath of her lungs, she seemed unable to move. She was in a kind of spellbound state, as though entranced by his kiss—waiting for him, utterly at his mercy; all she could do was pray without hope that he would be gentle with her.

He led her to the huge bed, and laid her on the wine-red coverlet, sitting beside her.

'You are so beautiful, Louise.' The deep voice was quiet, and she sensed, rather than felt, the tremor that underlay the husky purr. He stroked her cheek, and stared down into the green slits of her half-closed eyes. 'So graceful, so lovely . . .' His face was in half-shadow, the way it had been when she'd first seen him, that night of the party, when all the summer had seemed to be concentrated in that glassy, warm, evening sea.

She parted her lips helplessly under his kiss, the overwhelming irony of it all almost amusing her in a cruel way. But he was gentle, his mouth brushing the warm satin of her lips, tasting the moistness within, caressing the silken line of her throat. There was no way on earth she could control her reactions; it was as though some powerful electricity flowed directly from Bruno into her veins, changing everything within from ice into fire, from darkness into light. She arched to him, lifting her body to the elusive sweetness of his kiss. It was so easy to pretend that this was real, that nothing had ever happened between them; so easy to give way to the almost unbearable longing that his touch awoke in her, and to dream that this was a wedding-night, and not a goodbye.

She whispered his name, the words trailing off in a gasp as he drew his fingers across her flank to the swell of her breasts. Her arms were around his neck, drawing him close as if it were she who was the pursuer, the demanding one. Their kiss deepened, opening like a flower under midsummer sun to show the full colours of its beauty. The dark stars of her nipples hardened under his touch, ripening to an aching sensuality that was tenser, more urgent than anything she'd felt before. And the silence wrapped them in velvet arms.

The current in them now was strong, with the irresistible power of maturing emotion. The slow minutes were welding her to him, dizzily welcoming his weight as he sank down on to her. His lovemaking hardened from gentleness to rough, fierce imperiousness, commanding her response, forbidding her to disobey. The universe had become their bodies. Nothing else existed now but the sun of his desire, the peremptory caress of his fingers across her flanks, the soft inside of her thigh, the shivering skin of her stomach.

Louise fumbled blindly with his shirt, her fingers clumsy on the buttons until she could push the silk away, and caress his naked skin.

'Louise,' he shuddered, his arms tightening around her as her slender fingers explored the velvety warmth of his chest and the surging power of his shoulders, 'I want you, little bee . . .'

The endearment brought a sheen of tears to her eyes, reminding her so sharply of the relationship they'd had, the marvellous promise that had been blighted by her stupidity.

'You smell so sweet,' he groaned, his voice tormented. He kissed the silky valley between her breasts, where she'd touched herself with Opium hours, centuries, ago. 'This smell will always remind me of you——' Then all thought dissolved into a tumult of colour as his mouth brushed the aching point of her nipple, the moist warmth of his tongue bringing both torment and balm to her over-strained senses.

'Bruno,' she breathed, 'I adore you.'

The almost inaudible words seemed to stab him like a knife. He stiffened against her, freezing into immobility—then she called out in a low moan as he pulled abruptly out of her arms, and rolled away from her, his face grim.

Panting, she opened her dewy lashes to stare at him. The parted silk of his shirt showed muscles rigid with tension. 'What is it, my love?' she asked in bewilderment, reaching out to touch his face.

'I can't do this,' he grated, his eyes bleak. He brushed her hand away, and rose to his feet in one tight movement. She sat up, her mind still whirling with the passion he'd awakened in her.

'Bruno!'

'I can't stand it. You're doing it to me all over again, and I can't stand it.' He dug the heels of his hands into his eyes briefly, then walked to the moonlit window, his fists on his taut waist. His voice was uneven, rusty. 'You'll be relieved to hear that the comedy is over at last.'

'*Relieved*? But——'

'I can't bring myself to your level.' He turned to her, his mouth a savage line. 'I thought I could bring myself to take pleasure in your body, Louise—as a kind of recompense for what you did to me. But I find I can't.' He snatched his jacket up savagely, and slung it over his shoulder. 'You see, it's too much for me. You were toying with me—but I cared about you, woman.' Bitterness twisted his beautiful face. 'And I find I'm such a fool that I care for you still. More than I can bear. I'm going to get some air.'

'My love,' she cried, covering her breasts in shock, 'don't you think I feel——'

'I don't want to hear your blasphemies,' he snarled, his eyes glowing with a wolf's feral anger. 'God, how stupid I've been! To think I could hold you in my arms, kiss you, listen to that catch in your throat when I touch you—and not be moved!' His eyes devoured her pale face, framed with tousled hair, the honeyed curve of her body, and then he turned away, squeezing his eyes shut. 'Making love to you means too much to me to go through with it like this. I prefer to dream of how it might have been.' She stared wildly at him, her heart lacerated by the terrible irony of his words. 'You're like a drug in my bloodstream, woman,' he whispered, '—a fever that I can't cure. If only I could burn the memory of you out of my mind, tear the smell of your body from my senses——'

'But you can't see the truth,' she burst out, her voice trembling, 'you're blinded to reality! Now you know how much you care—can't you understand that I feel the same way?'

'*No,*' he rasped, the impact of his fury like a lash across her face. 'You don't give a damn!' He drew a deep, rasping breath. 'No,' he said again, gently, tiredly, 'you can't try the same trick twice, Louise. No man would be that much of a fool.'

'What must I do to show you how I feel?' she sobbed, unable to hold back the tears any more. 'My only darling, I've told you how sorry I am for what I did. I'd throw myself into the mouth of Etna if it would convince you of the truth——'

She choked on the words, and buried her face against the wine-red coverlet. She'd run out of words, run out of hope, run out of strength.

For a long while she simply wept, the tears seeping silently into the material, her mind an empty ache. When at last she had the courage to raise her wet face, Bruno was gone. The tide swayed *Merope* at her anchor, and no sound disturbed the deep stillness.

She awoke, haunted by nightmares, and sat up dazedly. She must have fallen asleep where she lay, her spirit emptied by the passions of the past hours. By the clock on the bedside table, it was four-thirty a.m. They'd spent the whole night locked in their torment, and outside, in the east, a flush of light heralded the coming dawn. She dressed, more tired than she'd ever been in her life.

Feeling crumpled and drained of emotion, Louise walked down the long, dark corridor, and silently pushed the door of the state room open. Bruno was alseep on the *chaise-longue*, his head thrown back against the velvet. She went to him, and stared down into his face. Even in sleep, his brows were drawn darkly, and there was pain etched on the passionate mouth she knew and loved so well.

'I'm sorry,' she said softly. 'I never meant to hurt you.' He didn't stir. His breathing was slow, even. She smiled painfully, and bent to kiss the warm lips as softly as she could. Delicate as the touch was, it made him tense in his sleep. He whispered her name roughly, then rolled on to his side, pillowing his cheek against his shoulder.

Feeling the tears dangerously close again, she went out into the cool air on the deck. The street-lights of Mazzaró glimmered across the sea. She walked to the stern, and looked down into the little dinghy that bobbed alongside the white launch. Would she be able to row herself ashore? It wasn't all that far. She could see the oars inside it, and her father had taken her rowing on Loch Lomond when she was a girl, so she had some experience. Surely he couldn't possibly object if she took the dinghy, and moored it at the pier at Mazzaró. The little boat was tugging at the painter, as though inviting her to go. Making up her mind, she tucked her bag under her arm, hauled on the nylon rope until the dinghy was underneath the metal rungs, and clambered cautiously down into it.

She unshipped the aluminium oars, which were reassuringly light, and struggled with the knot that secured the little boat until she'd got it undone, and dropped the end of the rope into the water.

It was not a pleasant sensation to discover that the dinghy was already drifting eagerly away from the motherly white shape of *Merope*. She scrambled to the seat, and dug the oars into the dark water. The fierce resistance of the current was another unpleasant surprise. She heaved the boat round so that it was pointing towards Mazzaró, and hauled on both oars. No sooner had she lifted them for the second stroke than the buoyant little craft was spinning out of control, and turning obstinately to face up-coast again.

Gritting her teeth, Louise started rowing as powerfully as she could. 'I thought the Mediterranean was supposed to be calm?' she muttered, fighting down the ominous realisation that she had not made a wise decision. Her hands and forearms were unpleasantly shaky after only a few pulls, and a hint of cramp was settling itself under her ribs. She paused for breath, and looked over her shoulder towards Mazzaró. To her horror, she had drifted almost half-a-mile up-coast already, and both Mazzaró and *Merope* were horribly far away.

Too far even for a shout for help—if she'd had the courage to do so.

The tide, she realised with sudden anger at her own stupidity. The tide had changed—Bruno had said so, earlier on! There wasn't any use trying to fight against it—she was drifting fast now, the dinghy gliding smoothly over the dark water. Her heart was thudding painfully as she sat down to consider her position. In her present despairing mood, it would be all too easy to give way to panic. Where would the tide take her? All the way to the straits of Messina? Surely not. In the darkness ahead was a sparkle of light—Giarre, she realised with a trickle of hope, where she'd eaten lunch and read her article for the first time. She stood up and checked more carefully—yes, the tide would probably deposit her on the beach at Giarre, or at least close enough to row ashore.

Slightly heartened, she sat down again. There really wasn't much option but to wait until the sea brought her to shore. *Merope* was only a string of pearls in the night now, far behind her. To the east, the dawn was beginning to spread a mother-of-pearl glimmer along the horizon. Ahead, where the sky was still dark, Etna glowed ruby-red.

For the first time since she'd awakened, she allowed her mind to return to the incidents of the night before. However terrible their experience had been, at least she knew one thing now—that he cared for her deeply. Whether that emotion would ever have become love was a foolish speculation, and one which it was far too painful for her to pursue. The whole thing was hopeless now, their relationship in smoking ruins.

She'd never felt like this before, this emptiness inside that left only cynicism and defeat in her heart. She'd been too young when her father died to really understand grief; it had been more like an absence than a separation to her, something which sobered her, made her more aware of herself and her life. Not like this— this emotional desert she found herself in now.

Floating helplessly like this, at the mercy of the current, was somehow appropriate. She smiled without humour. That was just the way she felt—rudderless, isolated, terribly alone. What would Bruno do when he woke and saw the dinghy gone? Shrug, and forget her? Go looking for her at Mazzaró, and work out what had happened to her when he didn't find the dinghy moored there?

It didn't really matter. Nothing could change the way ₑe felt about her now. The best thing for her to do ₓould be to pack her bags, and take the pieces of her ₑeart back to England. Take leave—even resign—from *Women Today* and take a long break somewhere in the ₒountry. Maybe even with her mother. They'd seen far ₚo little of each other since she'd started working, and ₕe thought of going back to her job sickened her. She ₜcked the oars under the seat, and settled herself as ₒomfortably as she could. She was in for a fairly long ₓait.

It was two and a half hours later, in fact, when she ₓaded through the shallows, Christine Sharpe's ex-ₚensive black dress hoisted unceremoniously around ₑr waist, and hauled the dinghy on to the beach. But ₙot at Giarre. The vagaries of the tide had carried her ₜt least three miles past the town, to a stretch of white, ₗeserted beach lined with prickly pears. The sun was ₐbove the sea, a crimson disc glorying the whole sky. It ₛtained the water blood-red, and gleamed on the ₜowering bulk of Etna which dominated the horizon a ₑw miles away. This might have been the first day of ₜreation, she thought, her heart lightening at the ₐlmost primaeval beauty of the scene.

Chance had landed her on one of the loveliest ₚeaches she'd yet seen in Sicily, and she wondered why ₜ hadn't become a resort, like Mazzaró. A handful of ₛeagulls would have completed the scene—but, ₛtrangely, not a bird was stirring. Their day off, ₚerhaps, she smiled wryly. She dried her long brown ₗegs with Sophie's scarf, making a mental apology, and ₕhoved the dinghy as far as she could out of the water's ₓay. Not a soul had been stirring in Giarre as she'd ₗrifted by; even the fishermen, notoriously early risers, had been asleep. There had been masses of black volcanic rock all along the coast since Giarre, and the walk back to the town promised to be gruelling—especially in elegant, thin-strapped sandals.

Wondering what on earth she looked like, but not having the heart to check in her compact, she clambered up the beach, and found a little rocky path among the flowering prickly pears which led toward Giarre, as far as she could tell. She was hungry enough to want to try one of the luscious-looking fruit, but she didn't have a knife, and the spines put her off. She brushed sand off her feet, and slid one sandal on, reflecting that she hadn't brought exactly suitable footwear.

A strange muzziness was making her vaguely unsteady on her feet. Strain and hunger, probably. She tugged the other sandal on, trying to clear her head. How odd she felt! What was the memory that was shoving its way so insistently against the door of her mind? A half-remembered dream? Something about pulling on a sandal, and a humming dizziness in her head——

Fear darkened her thoughts, and for a wild moment her mind began to spin like a top. There was a train coming, she had to get out of the way! Logic fought its way uppermost. Not a train. The rumble was growing hugely, shaking the earth under her feet. Her mind cleared to terror. The earthquake was severe enough to shake her to her knees, her sharkskin bag flying out of her fingers as she tried to steady herself. With insane clarity, she thought, *I must remember to tell Bruno that the gift really does work* ... The tall prickly pears were swaying as though in a high gale, rocks and stones sliding and rolling every which way, as though the whole earth had been possessed of some malevolent poltergeist. And unlike that day at the restaurant, it wasn't passing away.

She found herself sliding helplessly back on to the sand. And then the world exploded.

CHAPTER EIGHT

THE scarlet blaze at the mouth of Etna was brief, the sudden opening and closing of a titanic furnace door, followed by a gigantic black cloud that hurled itself upwards into the morning sky, expanding and spreading as it rose. It took almost a minute for the sound to reach her where she sprawled on the beach, wide-eyed and frozen. It shook the earth, a crash louder than the loudest thunder, rolling over the landscape like the chariot of some god, sprawling out across the sea into the distance. The hot blast of wind that followed immediately afterwards turned the beach into a whirlwind of sand, snapping some of the prickly pears off at their roots and whipping the sea into a turgid froth.

She cowered into the ground, closing her eyes against the lashing sand, and tried to pray. When she eventually raised her head, her mouth and hair gritty with sand, the wind had died down, and a continuous, heavy rumbling was shaking the earth, as though unimaginably huge machinery were moving somewhere far off. The brightness of the day was becoming dark with terrifying swiftness. She stared up at the vast black cloud still pouring out of Etna, and shook her head in stunned disbelief. The smoke was towering into the sky, half a mile, a mile high. As she watched, the mountain spat another crimson flare into the smoke-cloud, and the earth boomed in sympathy.

It was an awesome sight, too vast and majestic for

...er to be able to fit it into words yet. None of the photographs she had seen, the countless postcards sold at every shop in Taormina, had captured the awe-inspiring scale of an eruption. With the biggest crash yet, a great fountain of lava burst out of the cone, raining streams of flame around the slopes. She felt an almost primitive impulse to fall on her knees and cover her face, as someone in the Old Testament might have done.

The earthquakes were continuing, making the palms and prickly-pears rock, and precipitating miniature landslides all around. The cloud in the sky had spread with astonishing rapidity, looming almost overhead now, She scrambled to her feet, feeling very shaky, and looked around. The dinghy was gone; the blast had flipped it into the sea, and she couldn't even see where it had floated to.

'Damn,' she whispered, still not sure whether she was in any immediate danger yet; after all, Etna was eight miles away. It was now becoming overcast. A lurid twilight had settled over the morning as the vast cloud filled the sky. The up-currents from the sea were keeping it off the beach, but it was rolling heavily across the higher ground a bare few hundred yards away. Exactly along the path that her little track took. It occurred to her that in sparing the beach, the cloud had spared her life; volcanic gases, she knew, were deadly.

It also occurred to her, dimly, that her cameras were still in her hotel-room in Taormina. Ironic! And here she was with a grandstand seat. She thought miserably of the lost dinghy. It was distinctly possible that she was going to pay very heavily for her privileged view of this cosmic upheaval. Possibly with her life. She brushed

sand off her face, and then yelped as something
burned her arm vindictively. Ash! It was beginning to
billow down in a heavy grey rain, hot, gritty stuff
that stank of sulphur and charcoal and the bowels of
the earth. Definitely frightened now, she ran to the
water's edge, and crouched in the shallows, racking
her brains for an escape. She glanced at the vast slabs
of old, black lava that jutted out to sea from both
ends of the beach. There was no doubt that lava
could, and did, reach her little beach. Fate and the
tides had landed her at the closest possible point to
Etna along the whole coast! She winced in horror at
the thought of it; she would burst into flames on a
beach, become liquid glass long before the molten tide
reached her. But lava, she had been told, moved very
slowly. At a mile an hour, it might be ten hours
before the flow reached where she was. And by then
she'd have been rescued. Surely?

In fascination, she stared up at the volcano, fitfully
visible through the smoke and ash. The land was dark
now, like early evening, and the first eruption seemed
over. But there was a thin scarlet trickle making its way
down the cone, which had changed colour from white
to black. A thin scarlet trickle which would be, in
reality, a vast, sluggish river of molten rock, hot enough
to incinerate anything known to man. Restlessly, she
turned to the sea. At worst, she could take to the water
and swim her way to Giarre. Three miles? She bit her
lip. Or she could walk to the town, risking the heavy
black clouds of almost certainly poisonous gas on the
way.

She looked down, and gasped in shock as she saw
that her arms were grey, lifeless-looking and horrible.
She jumped to her feet, staring down at her body. Her

legs, Chris Sharpe's dress, all were coated in a fine dusting of ash. She waded into the sea, rinsing the gritty stuff off her body with revulsion. The surface of the sea itself was becoming an opaque, undulating sheet of grey. Hideous stuff, gritty to the touch, sharp as powdered glass when rubbed between the fingers. The translucent blue of the Mediterranean was turning to a murky brown. And a few fish, she noted with another twist of horror, had begun flopping desperately on the surface. The sharp dust would be clogging their gills, destroying the delicate breathing mechanism. Was the same fate going to overtake her? The inside of her mouth felt abraded already, and she imagined with horror what the pulverized glass would do to her lungs. She wrenched Sophie's white scarf from around her neck, and rinsed the sorry-looking thing as best she could in the water. Then she tied it round her mouth and nose, and sank back into the water.

'Oh, Bruno,' she whispered tearfully, 'send someone soon—*please*!'

The ash had darkened the sky now, flickering eerily purple as sheet lightning jumped from cloud to cloud. The rumble of the eruption seemed to have settled into a constant subterranean growl now, interrupted fitfully by explosions as more lava fountained out of the cone. Up to her chin in the sea, Louise could feel the tremor through the water. Awe and terror held her spellbound with equal strength. She had never anticipated that it would be like this, so—so *catastrophic*. What had she expected? Something like a giant Roman candle, pretty and safely disposed of once the fun was over? No wonder the people of Sicily dreaded the eruptions which so fascinated foreigners—Louise could imagine what this fearful ash-fall would be doing to people, cars, hospitals, houses, streets, washing, animals, the length and breadth of Sicily.

She thought of Dottore Pirandello, and the others at the research station at Adrano. Had they been able to predict the blast? Were they now dead or dying under the rain of fire and ash that Etna was pouring down on them? Pity for them, and for all living creatures trapped, like herself, by Etna's violence brought tears to her eyes.

And Bruno—he would be awake by now, watching the gigantic plume of smoke from the cool tranquillity of *Merope*'s deck. How long before he began to worry about her?

The ash kept falling, an apparently inexhaustible rain that turned the world and the sea grey, and began to drift in piles, blurring the edges of the monochrome landscape, and then obliterating the finer details, like some terrible snow. She kept splashing her face and arms, but the water itself was polluted, and her long hair was tangled and grimy, her mouth gritty. Chris Sharpe's dress was an unrecognisable ruin, and she would eagerly have changed it for the humblest boiler-suit—as long as it covered her shoulders and throat.

After twenty minutes, the ash-fall began to subside, and the sky lightened perceptibly as a brisk wind cleared a path through the darkness. From her place in the shallow water, Louise stared up at Etna with bleared, awe-struck eyes. The great black cloud still spewing from the cone was immense, the biggest thing she'd ever seen. It reached miles up into the sky, a vast, untidy mushroom that was ever-growing, ever-spreading. She rose, and waded ashore, avoiding the flopping fishes at the water's edge. It was good to be able to pull her scratchy mask off, and breathe freely. The stink of sulphur hung over everything still, and the once-white beach was ankle-deep in ash. Apart from the rumbling of Etna in the distance, a deathly hush hung over everything. She scanned the sea with gritty-feeling eyes. Even if Bruno guessed what had happened to her, would they know where to look for her?

She peered more closely at the mountain. Something else was happening on the slopes. Three separate streams were making their way downwards now, moving much faster than the lava. Mudflows, she realised with a chill. A moving wall of shattered stone, melted snow and ice, liquidised debris of all kinds. Mud had caused more damage to life and property than anything else at Krakatoa and Pompeii. It was much hotter than boiling water, and could move over a hundred miles an hour. The great cascades were gathering momentum as they poured down from the cone.

And it was all steep, rolling countryside between Etna and where she now stood.

'God help me,' she whispered. How long would it take to reach her? Minutes? An hour? And then her little beach would be obliterated by that monstrous river, and she herself would be just one of the thousand living things seared to a dreadful death in the holocaust. The flickering of hope that had arisen in her heart went out, leaving a grim despair. Her only chance now was the sea. Mud flowed a lost faster than she could run or walk—but if she swam out to sea, she might escape the rolling, boiling rivers that would soon be here. And risk death by drowning? Preferable to the horror of the mudflow, at least.

The three-pronged flow was advancing. Even from where she watched, miles away, she could see the terrible speed at which it moved. Already, it had reached the vegetation-line, obviously moving down vast channels carved out over the millennia. Channels which ended at her beach. God, what a death-trap! No wonder this beautiful spot had never become a tourist-resort despite its perfect site!

Altogether, the flow must be half a mile to a mile wide. It would be tearing up trees and boulders as it came, she knew, gathering strength as it devoured everything moveable in its path. Both Giarre to the north and Acireale to the south would be threatened; the citizens in outlying districts were probably being evacuated even now.

She walked slowly back to the water, the prospect of imminent death real to her for the first time since that strange muzziness had warned her of what was coming over an hour ago. Well, she thought grimly, her plans for her future might have to be postponed. Permanently. If only she hadn't parted from Bruno on such a horrible note . . .

She squatted in the shallow water again, flinching occasionally as the dying fish splashed frantically close to her. What a way to die, in this eerie, blasted place, filthy and unrecognisable in a tattered Paris dress that wouldn't offer the slightest protection from the terror that was coming!

The distant buzzing didn't register at first, but then she saw it, skimming along the horizon from the direction of Catania. She jumped up, hope surging desperately in her. An Air–Sea Rescue helicopter, its distinctive yellow fuselage stark against the black layers of cloud. She snatched up her scarf, and began to wave frantically as it approached. It was moving slowly, obviously on the look-out for stranded people like herself.

Tears of relief came to her eyes as it tilted, shifted direction abruptly, and soared towards her. The nightmare was over. Laughing and crying, she waved deliriously as it came towards her, the drone of its motor growing loud enough to drown out the distant rumble of Etna.

It wasn't slowing down. She ran on to the beach, and began waving again, more urgently. Disbelief made her falter as it became evident that the helicopter was going to pass her by a hundred yards. She screamed at the top of her lungs, semaphoring wildly. The machine soared past. She could see the cylindrical floats which enabled it to land in the water, caught a glimpse of the pilots' faces, searching in the opposite direction—and then it was droning past, banking to avoid the ash-clouds that would block its motors, heading towards Catania.

She sank to her knees, sobbing futile, bitter tears. How could they possibly have seen her, a grey thing scuttling along a grey beach so far below?

And the vast mud-flow was spreading down the mountainside towards her, tumbling trees and whole landscapes in its boiling torrent. Through her tears, hatred of the volcano flared up in her, hatred at the way it belittled life, the indifference with which it destroyed so much beauty.

The helicopter was already a mile away, drifting up the coast, just out of reach of the ash-cloud. Had they been looking for her? Searching, perhaps, for a little dinghy? It was far too late for her now, anyway. She could hear the mud-flow already, a frightening rumble. The liquid avalanche was less than five miles away, and travelling at over a mile a minute. She had to fight down the horrible panic that rose up in her. She would drown herself, she resolved shakily, rather than face that dreadful scalding death.

A hot buffet of wind reached her, ahead of the mud-flow. It carried a searing breath of sulphur. She could see it clearly; the three prongs had merged into two great streams, a wall of mud hundreds of feet high, tumbling trees and rocks, animals and earth, a catastrophic deluge like the last day on earth.

And the sky was darkening again as the ash-fall resumed. She returned to the water, desperately trying to remember some prayers. The smell of brimstone was overpoweringly strong now, nauseating and poisonous, and again that superheated, muddy breath licked hungrily at her from the advancing mud-flow, stronger than before. Amidst the rumble of its movement, she could hear a constant crackling, the sound of trees being uprooted and rocks being crushed into slime. In the swirling cloud overhead, the sheet-lightning had begun to flicker weirdly again, and the rain of ash deepened chokingly.

The air was becoming hot enough to scorch her delicate skin, and even the sea was warm, its gritty surface littered with dead and dying fish. Louise tied her mask round her mouth and nose with trembling fingers, wading towards the deeper, cooler water. She was helplessly crying now, unable to control her despair. Her body was coated in the gritty grey slime, her arms and torso like a savage's, inhuman-looking. The water couldn't rinse it off, and it was horrible to feel dying creatures squirming against her in the sea. As she would soon be dying, too. Earth, sea and sky were filthy and poisoned, loud with savage noises; the darkness was terrifying, like some ancient plague, deepening all around her until only the flickering of the lightning and the dim, red glow of Etna were visible.

When she heard the hoarse voice calling her name, she at first thought it was some illusion, an hallucination brought on by her extremity. But she heard it again, closer now, and turned blindly towards the sound.

'Is anyone there?' she called, her voice choked with ash. The rumbling of the mud-flow was huge now, shaking the sea-bed under her feet, and there was no answer. Faint and dizzy, she swam towards the open sea, the massive heat of the mud blasting over her back.

Suddenly, something drifted out of the darkness across the smoking water towards her. Amazement conquered her despair. A tall grey man in a grey boat, some terrible spirit of this Godforsaken place——

'Louise!'

Above the thunder of the approaching mud, she recognised Bruno's voice. He was reaching grey hands out to her, leaning over the gunwale.

'For God's sake,' he roared into her dazed ears, 'take my hands!' An eruption of joy made her thrash wildly towards him. Bruno! He had come for her! His hands were steel-strong as he hauled her roughly into the boat, ignoring her incoherent babble. She sprawled in the bottom of the launch like a broken bird; he knotted fierce fingers in her hair, and pulled her face to his. 'Are you hurt?' he shouted above the vast rumble. She shook her head tearfully, trying to touch his face with slimy fingers. He sprang to the motor.

'Got to get going before the mud reaches us,' he shouted. 'I had to switch the engine off in case you were calling—but now this damned ash——'

The motor made no response to his jab at the ignition. She sat up weakly, still trying to grasp the reality of his presence. He wrenched one of the canopies open, and raked clogged ash off the air-filter. This time the motors exploded into vibrating life. Searing heat rushed over them, a breath from Hell-mouth itself, and he gunned the motor mercilessly, spinning the launch in a tight curve to point out to sea.

The noise of the avalanche reached an unbearable roar. She looked back, wild-eyed, to see her little beach disappear under an unbelievably high wall of death—boulders, mud and the churning roots of great trees, moving with terrifying speed down the slopes and into the water. The shrivelling heat clawed out at them, the racing mud-wall towering over the launch, the air becoming unbreathable with the stench of sulphur.

Bruno was accelerating as hard as he dared, the screws digging desperately at the gritty water; and with agonising slowness, the launch began to outdistance the wall of mud. The avalanche was subsiding into the sea with a deafening roar, the shock-wave itself helping to hurl the launch onwards. Turbulent grey fingers reached massively around them. An agonisingly scorching heat surged under the boat, dragging a scream from Louise's lungs. He turned from the wheel and grasped her wrist, pulling her against his hard body—and then they were hurtling into the mist towards open sea, leaving the stink and the roar behind them.

Clinging to him, Louise felt the cool wind blow the raging heat off her skin. The ash-cloud billowed around them as the launch buffeted its way across the sea, towards the only light they could see. She lay against him, her face pressed to his neck, her heart too full for words. The air cleared slowly as the minutes passed, and as the last shreds of the ash-cloud began to whip past them, the launch rode out into the clear blue skies of a summer morning.

They turned to one another, two scarecrow figures, hideous with ash. She didn't even have the strength to smile.

The last thing Louise felt was Bruno's supporting arm as she slid bonelessly against the seat, her overstrained body finally giving up the unequal struggle with exhaustion.

It was cool evening by the time she drifted out of her dreams. She knew instinctively where she was; she didn't have to check the coverlet round her to know that it was wine-red. The yacht was moving gently on the tide, and it was deeply peaceful, only the murmur of the sea disturbing the immense quiet. She stretched luxuriously, blissfully aware that her skin felt smooth and clean. Still half-asleep, she ran her fingers through her hair. It was silky, tumbled around her face in scented disarray. She smiled sleepily, thinking that someone had done a good job on the ghastly mess she must have been.

She blinked into wakefulness, and sat up. Twilight was flooding the luxurious cabin. The sky was violet and salmon and ultramarine outside. She was naked, though some professional hand had bandaged cuts and abrasions on her arms and fingers.

'Bruno . . .' she whispered. He had come looking for her, risking his own life to find her. Tenderness flooded her, a deep love that was more profound than any emotion she'd ever felt before. It erased the horror of the past hours, filling her soul with the urgency of her need for Bruno. She climbed stiffly out of bed, aware of aches and pains all over her body, and pulled on the white gown which had been left on the chair. In the mirror she saw a rather pale face, framed with tumbled, glossy hair, the green eyes still dreamy with sleep. But she didn't bother trying to adjust her appearance. She needed to see him much too badly.

She padded on bare feet down the corridor, and softly pushed the state room door open. He turned to her from the window where he'd been standing, and their eyes met across the softly lit room. His smile was slow, gentle.

'You slept well?'

She nodded, not trusting herself to speak. He was magnificent in the dim light, the dark blue robe emphasising the grandeur of his big frame.

'The doctor who dressed your wounds tells me you're going to live.' She nodded again, walking on to the exquisite Persian rug, aching to dissolve into his arms, yet too shy, too uncertain to do more than smile timidly. He turned to the desk, and picked up the crimson-bordered copy of *Women Today*. 'I've been reading your article,' he said casually.

Her voice was husky. 'Oh. And what do you think?' The dark eyes met hers again, bringing that old electricity surging into her veins.

'I think you love me,' he said softly.

'Oh, yes,' she whispered, her heart contracting painfully inside her. 'I love you, Bruno. I always have done.'

He reached out his hand to her, his expression unreadable.

'Come.'

She walked with him on to the deck. The evening was silent. To the north, though, an immense pall of smoke rose in a huge pillar into the heavens, seeming to reach the stars themselves. The cone of Etna was silhouetted against the violet sky, and a long, glimmering ribbon of scarlet lay against one flank, a stream of lava almost a mile wide and eight miles long, reaching from the high cone to the sheen of the sea.

'It's beautiful,' she breathed, drinking in the fantastic sight.

'Beautiful,' he agreed. 'Your friends are all dying to see you. I suggested tomorrow morning as a suitable visiting-time. In the meantime, they're getting the most exciting stories and photographs of their career—including your narrow escape. And you didn't get a single picture.'

'And I had a front-row seat,' she nodded wryly. 'Percy will kill me.'

'Not unless he wants to face me,' Bruno smiled. 'I telephoned your Mr Widows this afternoon.'

'Oh!' she said, her heart sinking. 'About—about my article?'

'No. Simply to explain why you weren't going to be sending any pictures in. Oh,' he added casually, 'and to arrange six months' leave for you.'

'Six months' leave?' she faltered, not sure whether he was joking or not.

'Sure. If I'd been a high-handed man, I might have tendered your resignation. But I thought I'd let you think about that yourself.' There was gentle laughter in his voice. He was standing behind her, and now he drew her close against his chest, his arms encircling her tightly, possessively. His deep voice was close to her ear. 'Forget all that now. Look at the pretty volcano.'

Revelling in his touch, she caressed his big hands with slender fingers, her mind spinning. 'How did you know where to find me?'

'Beppo knew. He knew where the current would take you on that tide. I almost had to fight him to stop him coming with me, I might add. He is a brave man—but I could not risk his life as well as yours and mine.'

'If you hadn't found me when you did,' she said, leaning her head dreamily against his chest, 'the mud would have reached that beach, and you——'

'My little bee,' he said softly into the silence she left, 'if I hadn't found you, I'd never have left that beach.'

'Don't say that,' she said in a low, urgent voice. 'I'm not worth dying for!'

'You're worth living for,' he smiled. 'The only thing in my world worth living for. And when there's no purpose to life—why, then it's easily ended.' He turned her in his arms, silencing her protests with a touch on her lips. 'And I would have deserved no less. It would have been I who had sentenced you to that cruel death.' He took her face in his hands reverently, caressing the rich, dark clouds of hair away from her mouth and eyes. 'How could I have been such a fool, Louise?' he said, his deep voice low and rough. 'Dear God, how blind I was!'

'I was the fool,' she said, smiling shakily. 'If you could only put down what I did to inexperience, and give me another chance——'

'Hush,' he commanded, his eyes smoky on hers, the tender desire in them melting her very bones. 'Tell me, little bee, are you ever going to be able to forgive me? All the time that I was looking for you among the ash and the smoke, I was thinking back to everything I'd said to you since yesterday. All the cruel things I said, all the cruel things I did—it was a revelation to me. A revelation of how blind and foolish an arrogant man can be.'

'Bruno,' she said, half-way between laughter and tears, 'we've both been such fools, so blind—but no more talk of forgiveness. Such things don't have a place in our lives any more . . .'

His lips sealed the words against her lips, his kiss like hot wine poured into her blood, intoxicating her body and soul. She clung to his hard shoulders, her lips parting under the fierce heat of his need for her. There was awe in her half-closed green eyes as she looked up into his face afterwards. 'I don't know what I've done to deserve you,' she whispered, tracing the passionate, commanding line of his mouth with unsteady fingers, 'but I thank God for it, my darling.'

'If we all got what we deserved,' he smiled gently, 'humanity would be a tragic thing. But some Providence sees to it that we are rewarded far, far beyond our deserts. As I am with you,' he whispered, punctuating the words with a kiss, 'despite the terrible, criminal mistake I made in misjudging you. The mistake which so nearly——' He stopped, unable to say the words, and drew a deep breath. 'Anyway,' he grinned, 'it's wonderful to know that I'm going to be marrying——'

'Marrying?'

'Marrying,' he emphasised, caressing her satiny lips with his own, 'not only a beautiful, sensitive, sexy woman, but a brilliant writer, too. I read your article three times, while you slept, Louise. And I think it's one of the most poetic and tender things I've ever seen. Don't interrupt,' he warned, hushing her words. 'Let me finish. In my blind, proud fury, I was so certain that what you'd done was a repeat of the Ackermann episode that I barely read your text.' There was a touch of the old irony in his oblique smile. 'You make me out to be very glamorous, my love. Much more so that I can ever possibly be. And I don't think anyone reading that article can be in much doubt about your feelings towards your subject.'

She laid her cheek against his chest, smiling wryly. 'It's unfair to hold a woman in love responsible for what she writes,' she murmured.

'Your little exaggerations about me aside,' he said quietly, 'I know what a great gift you have. I also know that you're far too talented and sensitive to be working for a silly, glossy thing like *Women Today* all your life. You should be writing books—books about travel, about life, about love, about the world as you see it through those bewitchingly beautiful, compassionate green eyes. But in the name of God,' he said, laughing huskily at the expression on her face, 'no more about me, woman!'

'Oh, Bruno——'

'To hell with these absurd garments,' he muttered, his deep voice urgent with desire, 'I need to touch your skin——' He unfastened her robe with impatient fingers, then his own, and drew her fiercely against him. The seamless contact of their naked bodies wrenched a gasp of passion from her, her eyes fluttering helplessly closed as his mouth claimed hers with an utter, complete possession more eloquent than any words. She was his—his for ever, his so totally that not even death would part them . . .

'Stop,' she pleaded in a trembling whisper, the naked thrust of his desire dizzying her mind, intoxicating her senses, 'I want to talk to you—so many things to say——'

'Later,' he growled, the deep vibrancy in his voice promising the fullness of the passion to come. 'We've got the rest of our lives to talk in. Wonderful, beautiful lives. And I've been waiting all afternoon for this, while you were sleeping——' His mouth was hot, demanding against her throat, the silky skin of her neck, her breast . . .

'What are we going to do?' she pleaded ecstatically, her dreamy voice so soft that she wasn't sure he'd even heard her.

'You mean—after this?' he grinned wickedly, deep grey eyes devouring her face.

'Yes!'

'I thought we'd fly to London, and see your mother. My family has made the mistake of not seeking parental permission once too often, little bee.'

'Are you sure you want to marry me——?'

The question was punished by a ruthlessly fierce kiss which melted slowly into heart-stopping tenderness.

'Don't ask such things,' he said roughly, worshipping her with wondering eyes. 'You're the light of my life, Louise. I'll never let you go again, not so far as the other end of the street!'

He picked her up in powerful arms, carrying her down the corridor to the wine-red bed she'd so recently arisen from.

'And after that,' he continued, 'a quiet wedding in some local church. And then a honeymoon. Starting in Abondance.' He laid her on the bed, smiling down into her drugged eyes. 'I've been working much too hard for years, Louise. Now my business can get along without me for a year or two, while I feast my soul on——' he brushed the soft white robe aside, and gazed down on her honey-tanned body, '—you.'

'And then?' she whispered, glorying in the hunger for her so evident in those smoky grey eyes, the hunger she knew could never be satisfied.

'And then,' he smiled, laying his hand on her womb, 'When you are ready, we shall go home, and make *Le Faucon* blossom once more.'

In the distant night, Etna's spectacular beauty glimmered like some primitive magic, a pagan spell that enriched the earth with fiery life.

But here on the immense peace of the sea, the two people whom its enchantment had welded together for ever neither saw nor cared.

An epic novel of exotic rituals
and the lure of the Upper Amazon

THE TAKERS RIVER OF GOLD

JERRY AND S.A. AHERN

THE TAKERS are the intrepid Josh Culhane and the seductive Mary Mulrooney. These two adventurers launch an incredible journey into the Brazilian rain forest. Far upriver, the jungle yields its deepest secret—the lost city of the Amazon warrior women!

THE TAKERS series is making publishing history. Awarded *The Romantic Times* first prize for High Adventure in 1984, the opening book in the series was hailed by *The Romantic Times* as "the next trend in romance writing and reading. Highly recommended!"

Jerry and S.A. Ahern have never been better!

TAK – 3

A Gold Eagle book from Worldwide, available now wherever
Harlequin and Silhouette paperbacks are sold

Share the joys and sorrows of real-life love with

Harlequin American Romance!™

GET THIS BOOK FREE

as your introduction to **Harlequin American Romance** — an exciting series of romance novels written especially for the American woman of today.

Mail to:
Harlequin Reader Service

In the U.S.	In Canada
2504 West Southern Ave.	P.O. Box 2800, Postal Station A
Tempe, AZ 85282	5170 Yonge St., Willowdale, Ont. M2N 5T5

YES! I want to be one of the first to discover **Harlequin American Romance.** Send me FREE and without obligation *Twice in a Lifetime.* If you do not hear from me after I have examined my FREE book, please send me the 4 new **Harlequin American Romances** each month as soon as they come off the presses. I understand that I will be billed only $2.25 for each book (total $9.00). There are no shipping or handling charges. There is no minimum number of books that I have to purchase. In fact, I may cancel this arrangement at any time. *Twice in a Lifetime* is mine to keep as a FREE gift, even if I do not buy any additional books. **154 BPA NAZJ**

Name _____ (please print)

Address _____ Apt. no.

City _____ State/Prov. _____ Zip/Postal Code

Signature (If under 18, parent or guardian must sign.)

This offer is limited to one order per household and not valid to current Harlequin American Romance subscribers. We reserve the right to exercise discretion in granting membership. If price changes are necessary, you will be notified.

AMR-SUB-1